———————— ★ ————————

In one of those little huts on the allotments, just
passed by John Coffin, the Paper Man was at work.
He was laboriously putting together an archive. He
typed slowly with one hand.

DEATH NUMBER ONE, he typed.

Then he added the date, and the quantity of poison used. Not where he had obtained the poison,
that would be telling.

Then he rolled up what he had written in a plastic
sheet and, like a dog, he buried it.

Like a dog, he knew exactly where he had buried it.
Would dig it up when needed, and had left minute
signs, but careful ones, where it could be found.

You might find it yourself.

———————— ★ ————————

# COFFIN
## AND THE
# PAPER MAN

## Gwendoline Butler

# W🌐RLDWIDE.

TORONTO • NEW YORK • LONDON
AMSTERDAM • PARIS • SYDNEY • HAMBURG
STOCKHOLM • ATHENS • TOKYO • MILAN
MADRID • WARSAW • BUDAPEST • AUCKLAND

**COFFIN AND THE PAPER MAN**

A Worldwide Mystery/December 1993

First published by St. Martin's Press, Incorporated.

ISBN 0-373-26133-0

Copyright © 1990 by Gwendoline Butler.
All rights reserved. No part of this book may be reproduced or transmitted in any form or by any means, electronic or mechanical, including photocopying, recording or by any information storage and retrieval system, without permission in writing from the publisher. For information, contact: St. Martin's Press, Incorporated, 175 Fifth Avenue, New York, NY 10010-7848 U.S.A.

All characters in this book are fictitious, and any resemblance to actual persons, living or dead, is purely coincidental.

® and TM are trademarks of Harlequin Enterprises Limited. Trademarks indicated with ® are registered in the United States Patent and Trademark Office, the Canadian Trade Marks Office and in other countries.

Printed in U.S.A.

# COFFIN
## AND THE
## PAPER MAN

# ONE

*The Day of May 25 and on to May 27*

GRIM. GRIM. the word was going out over the police airwaves at Nineteen hundred hours precisely on this day, May 27, 1989.

GRIM. GRIM. Rope Alley, Leathergate.

THIS WAS THE code word in the police district under the command of John Coffin (thought intellectual and elusive by his new Force, where his code name was WALKER, but never judged arrogant or uncaring), for what they were beginning to call gender murders.

Gender murder: the killing of a woman in circumstances of a sexual assault. GM. Because the word rape came up, the letter R got itself into the code.

The code was beginning to creep into use all over the many areas and peoples that make up modern London. The two Londons, the many Londons.

London is a collection of villages. They stretch out on either side of the river into the flat lands of Essex, and up towards the hills of Kent.

Some are very old with their names in the Domesday Book and even earlier records. Such are Wapping and Billingsgate and Greenwich. Under other names, the Romans probably knew them too and cursed them for being barbaric and remote from the warmth and comforts of their home town. Some, like Mayfair, are relatively new. New as these things go, owing their existence to the shift of fashion westwards from the old city clustered around the Tower. Interestingly, the centres of crime have shifted westward with the centuries, keeping in touch with fashion.

Most of the villages are happy ones, but some are happier than others and one or two are unhappy. For various reasons.

The old village of Leathergate was very unhappy at the moment. It had known some rough times in the past, when murder and violent death had been almost a home industry, but the present days were uneasy, with the new rich in their smart new apartments irritating the old poor, while the new poor, some of whom had known better days, were even crosser. A mini war of the classes was brewing up in Leathergate.

Leathergate was part of the new Second City of London whose policing was in the hands of the new Force directed by John Coffin, Chief Commander. Together with Spinnergate, and Swinehouse and Easthythe and other old villages both south and east, it was a whole new urban concept. Old in history but with a new Royal Charter and lots of hopes.

In Leathergate that May 25, a girl lay dying in an alley.

She had been beaten and raped, and then a knife had penetrated her ribs, cutting through to her lungs. She did not die at once.

She was still alive when a boy with his dog discovered her, still alive as the ambulance arrived.

She spoke to the ambulance men.

'Get the man who killed me,' she whispered.

The ambulance driver, a senior man, turned to his junior. 'Lift her up carefully, she's going to go.'

They were always careful, it was his emotion that spoke. He knew the girl.

At that moment, she died.

Anna Mary Kinver was sixteen years old, looking eighteen. She had long fine blonde hair which was tangled and bloody in the mud. The same mixture, red and black, spread over her check mini skirt and white shirt. It was the day before her birthday when she had a party planned at a local disco and in the alley beside her was her new party dress for next day and a pair of silver slippers, one of which was missing.

Poor little Cinderella who would never get to the ball. Rope Alley ran between the old Clover Rope Works, now converted into smart apartments, and the former Lead Works, now an art gallery. It is as well to get the geography right in this complicated district with its palimpsest of history.

The narrow path between the two high buildings was the way home between the shops in the North Ferry Road and Elder Street.

Anna Mary Kinver, one of the new poor, descended from a long line of the old poor, had lived with her father, new poor/old poor nicely mixed up, in a house in Elder Street. He was there now, waiting for her to come home. She was never going to come.

A policewoman knocked on the door of No. 13. She too had known Anna Mary Kinver, having been in the top class of the last comprehensive when Anna Mary had arrived, a skinny eleven-year-old, to be educated into believing that there was a rich world outside into which, if she learnt French, German, mathematics and how to use a computer, she could be inserted. Thus she was rich, then poor, almost at once afterwards.

Still rich in hope and expectations on the day she died, but poor in any practical delivery of what she wanted, and only able to afford a pair of silver slippers from Mr Azzopardi's Bazaar rather than from Maud Frizon in Bond Street. She knew about Maud Frizon though, and had stared in the window at her pretty shoes.

The policewoman hated the task she had been given. It was monstrous, horrible, and sad. But it was her job and she was going to do it.

She did not mention death as she first spoke to Fred Kinver, she just spoke of a bad accident and the hospital. She would get round to the rest of the message as she drove him to where he must go.

If he hadn't guessed. People did guess.

The exact circumstances of Anna's death had been passed on to the WPC by her sergeant, but these she would not transmit. He'd find out soon enough.

She meditated for a moment on the fact that he would have to identify the body. Oh dear. Fred Kinver was not going to be able to bear doing that, but he would have to. He had the look of one of those who would turn aside from a dead rabbit. She was not unlike that herself, but after several professional visits to the police mortuary she had learnt the knack of not seeing more than you must.

Of course, for him that would be difficult.

Fred Kinver sat beside her in the police car, having a pretty shrewd idea of what lay before him. He had that sick feeling in the pit of his stomach that assured him that the worst had happened.

'The wife's out,' he said. 'Hasn't got back from her work. She has an evening job. I shall have to tell her later.'

'We'll do that for you, Mr Kinver.'

'Better do it myself.'

We'll see, thought the WPC. See how you feel.

Fred Kinver had worked in the biscuit factory in Deen Street till it moved to Slough, somehow managing to let Mr Kinver float away from it. Then he had worked in a small bakery until that was swallowed up by a supermarket. He had gone free from that too, although several other employees had been taken on. To encourage the fresh-bread-baking smell over the wrapped bread counter, the cynics said. Since then he had done odd jobs around the new local theatre, the Theatre Workshop founded by Mrs Lætitia Bingham, where his wife worked for one of the actresses as dresser cum handywoman.

Anna Mary had been studying computer programming at the local Sixth Form College with a grant from the City firm which had promised her a job on completion. The grant was a good one, more than her father earned in a year, so that he called her one of the rich. But the Crash of '87 with the doldrums that followed had obliged the firm to declare redundancies. Anna Mary lost her grant and her offer of a job. So she was one of the new poor before truly she had ever been one of the new rich, it had all been hopes and dreams. But at her age, she said, it didn't matter, and she loved dancing at discos where she had any number of friends.

WPC Flo Rusher, Flurry to her friends, drove carefully towards the newly built police headquarters, taking back streets like Pavlov Street and Down Road and Peterloo Circus, to avoid the traffic. Nice area, she thought, live around here if I could.

'Nearly there.'

'Remember what this was like in the old days?' asked Fred Kinver as if it mattered to him.

'Not really.' She swerved expertly round an illegally parked Porsche. She knew Mr Kinver although he didn't seem to know her. Broken Biscuits, they'd called him. Anna Mary had always had a bag of broken biscuits in her pocket.

'Slums. Packed little houses. Full of people and mice. But friendly. Look at it now. Too bloody rich to speak to the world.'

She looked at his thin hands twisting restlessly in his lap. This is going to be one of the really bad ones, she thought.

Fred Kinver suddenly sat up alertly. 'Wait a minute, this isn't the way to the hospital.'

How to tell him that his daughter had died as the ambulance men touched her, and would therefore have been DOA and hence not taken to the hospital but to the police mortuary? Or for all Flurry knew, she might still be *in situ* in Rope Walk, being measured and photographed.

'Not just at the moment, Mr Kinver,' she said soothingly. 'Our DI wants a word with you first.'

Suddenly aware of what lay ahead of him, Fred Kinver began to scream.

IN ONE OF HIS rare moments of leisure, John Coffin had speculated that the so-called Second City of London together with his new Force had been invented to annoy him. His patch was ripe with murders and crimes of violence, rich in sophisticated villainy. Had been for centuries, they had nothing to learn.

Two days after the murder of Anna Mary, on May 27, in the course of one of his unscheduled and unannounced forays of inspection around his new headquarters he had seen the report on Anna Mary.

Not one of our better jobs, he thought, but routine for round here. The thought did not cheer him up. He had gone through a lot since he took up his new command. Too much, perhaps.

To his surprise, however, he had no more grey hairs and was no thinner now than two years ago when he had been appointed. Perhaps his expression was more cautious.

'You look so canny these days, John,' his half-sister Letty Bingham had said only that morning, Saturday, May 27. She had called from New York where she was visiting her husband. Or so Coffin supposed; his name was never mentioned and possibly had long since been banished. It was not a subject he was going to raise with his sister, especially on the telephone, where he was always frugal. But time and distance made no difference to Letty when telephoning, she would call as readily from the States as from across London and talk as long in the small hours as at noon.

'That's because I'm always watching my rear.'

'As good soldiers do. And you're a good soldier, John.'

'Think so? And a good politician too, I hope, because I have to be that as well.'

They shared the same mother but had different fathers and had experienced vastly different upbringings. Letty, offspring of a GI father, had been educated in English schools and an American university. She was a lawyer, and had been married twice. Coffin wondered about the state of this second marriage to a property magnate of some wealth, but, granted they never seem to be in the same continent together, it seemed to be holding.

Letty had a daughter, and both of them shared another half-brother called William who was a Writer to the Signet in Edinburgh.

After years of thinking himself alone in the world, Coffin now found himself with respectable family connections. And remarkably, as he had pointed out, they all seemed attracted to the law in one way and another, so there had to be something in ancestry after all.

Their elusive mother who had bred them all, choosing her mates eclectically, was dead, but her presence lingered on in the shape of some amazing diaries that Letty Bingham declared should be published.

Over my dead body, Coffin thought. A certain theatricalism hung over Mother's memoirs and this quality had rubbed off on Letty (possibly all lawyers had it), who was now engaged in turning a piece of property, an old church owned by her husband in the New City, into a theatre and a theatre workshop.

The workshop was in operation, the theatre was still on the planning board, but the luxury flats which were meant to help pay the way of the theatre were complete and occupied.

John Coffin lived in one, and although he had flinched at the cost of his apartment in the tower of old St Luke's Church, he now enjoyed living there very much. He liked looking down from his high window on the world below where he must keep the Queen's Peace.

There were two other tenants, one of whom, the actress Stella Pinero, he knew very well, and the other, recently moved in, he had not yet met. A man, so he was told. An art dealer, rumour had it, who had bought the Lead Works Art Gallery. Ot was it his friend who had bought the flat, Sir Harry Beauchamp? Rumour and invention were still working on the story.

Letty had made money on all that enterprise, but she was now much preoccupied with creating her theatre, which was why she had telephoned.

'I want to call it the Ellen Terry. What do you think of that? We must get the name settled soon because of the publicity.' Letty always thought about the publicity, good or bad. Any was better than none, she believed.

'Have you asked Stella? She usually has good ideas.'

'I think Stella is more worried about the lavatories at the moment,' said Letty tartly. 'She's always so practical.'

Stella Pinero, that distinguished actress, had accepted the appointment as resident director of the Theatre Workshop, with the implied assumption that she would continue with the main theatre when built. Times away from other work in TV and films and the other companies had been carefully negotiated, and she had just finished a six months' stint on the West End stage in a long-running comedy and was back to appear in the Workshop Theatre, richer and ready for a change.

'I've got to live,' she had pointed out to Letty, 'and what you pay wouldn't keep a cat alive.' She had a cat, as it happened, or a half share, as Tiddles lived part-time with John Coffin.

'I thought it was security that worried her.' Letty Bingham's enterprise in converting the disused St

Luke's Church into several luxury apartments, together with a Theatre Workshop and the planned main theatre, was popular in the district as bringing lustre on the neighbourhood, but lately a certain Them and Us attitude had marred the good will.

Stella had not liked having GO HOME YUPPIE painted all over her posters for her last production, *The Birthday Party*, and a load of rubbish deposited outside the stage door. Nor having one of her cast beaten up on his way home.

'That too, but she feels happier now she's got Bovvy End on her team as assistant director; he's so huge she feels he ought to be able to protect them against most things.'

Though you can't be protected against everything, thought Coffin, his mind going back to the latest murder in Leathergate.

'Anyway, I am flying back tonight,' said Letty. 'That's why I am telephoning. How are you getting on with Mother?'

'I've read most of her production. Her handwriting is terrible, though. Slows me down.'

'I suppose she did mean it as truth? Has it occurred to you it might be a work of fiction?'

'I think she was a bit of a liar, our mother, if that's what you mean.'

A liar and an escape artist as well: she had produced three children by three separate fathers and managed to abandon them all.

'There's a very interesting murder going on here,' ended Letty conversationally. 'A girl's head in a bathtub, and bits of her turning up everywhere. They're looking for her feet now. I declare I'll be glad to be back in London.'

We have our murders too, thought Coffin, as Letty's presence (he could nearly always see Letty when they spoke, she seemed able to project herself visually) in his room melted back across the Atlantic. And I'm looking for a shoe.

Since he had to speak to DI Young on other business (they were both on a committee setting up an under-fifteen football club in the old Brush Lane ground down by Beowulf Dock), he was able to ask: 'And have you found the other silver shoe?'

'Not as yet. But we will.' DI Young sounded confident. As he always did. He had decided early on in his career that this was the right way to appear and so far had seen no reason to change his attitude. At home was different: his wife was smarter than he was, better educated and was climbing up the career ladder (she too was a police officer) faster than he was. At home he was more cautious.

Coffin nodded. 'Let me know. I'll be interested.'

'Right, sir.' Cheerful as ever, Archie Young had added: 'We'll soon have the whole thing wound up. Several interesting leads. A witness who saw a man near her. A woman who heard her call out. Didn't do anything, of course, but heard her. That gives us time. And then there's what she said herself.'

*Get the man who killed me.*

Yes, that was interesting. But how did it help?

'We know it was a man, anyway,' he said to Young. 'It means she didn't know him.'

He was pleased with himself. Got the old man there, he thought.

But John Coffin, as he put the receiver down, picked up his briefcase, and patted the cat, thought: I wonder. I wouldn't count on anything. Long experience had taught him, what was it, canniness?

Archie Young was sharp enough to pick up the implications of his boss's voice. 'I have the names of her friends from A to Z,' he said to the well-filtered air of his office.

BEHIND THE big new police station which was the Force Headquarters and which had been designed by a neo-modernist architect so that it looked like a Venetian Gothic castle in red brick (but was bulletproof and fireproofed and so air-conditioned that not one natural breath could be drawn in it) was what had once been the choicest area of Leathergate in which to live. The street where the few professionals like the doctor and the solicitor and the undertaker had made their homes. It was still a nice district and a few of the old families clung on.

Feather Street curved down a gentle slope and up the other side until it looked down on the railway embankment, solid Victorian houses with large gardens which backed on to each other so that cats, dogs and even humans could pass freely between them. At the bottom of the hill were a few shops such as a dairy, and a baker's and a shop renting videos out.

Here still lived Dr Leonard Zeman, his wife Felicity, who was a pediatrician, and his son Tim, who was an architectural student at the Poly. Across the way was the house of his widowed mother and her unmarried niece. The Zeman houses were No. 5 and No. 22 respectively. Felicity had a white pekinese dog and her mother-in-law had a mongrel called Bob.

The Annecks were the owners of No. 10 and the Darbyshires lived in No. 13. They had Jack Russell

terriers, brother and sister, who hated the sight of each
other, fought whenever they could and had to be ex-
ercised separately at different hours. The families had
worked out a rota of dog departures and entrances and
a bell was rung before setting out to make sure the en-
emies did not meet. They were suspected of having
killed a cat apiece. These were the families that knew
each other best in Feather Street. Mrs Anneck was a
local councillor, Harold Darbyshire worked in the
Bank, and everyone knew Dr Zeman.

They were all very busy people, fond of their animals but not good at exercising them, so they were
walked accordingly to a strict timetable by Jim Marsh,
the son of the milkman (C. Marsh, Daily Deliveries,
who had not always been a milkman but had been into
Flower Power and Love is All and being a Free Soul,
only a man must live), who was hoping to be a vet. He
was a kind of professional dog-walker, and, as a matter of fact, it was he who had found Anna Mary's
body. With him at that time was the better behaved of
the Jack Russells, but even so he had had to pull back
the dog from licking at the blood on the pavement.

The dog-walker was a quiet, thin boy, over eighteen but looking younger, who loved the dogs, but even
he found this hard to bear. When he got home, he was
sick in the kitchen sink before preparing a meal for his
father. His mother was dead.

The policeman who had brought him home had
been kind but not really understanding. The ride in the
police car had been interesting, although not enjoyed
by the dog he was walking.

'You know, Mum,' he said—he still spoke to his
mother sometimes, although she had been dead some

months now, and she seemed to pay more attention than she had in the past. 'It was bad. Bad.'

He too had heard the words that Anna Mary had spoken.

COFFIN having completed his call to Archie Young, prepared to depart for yet another committee meeting, this time one he would chair. He was a desk man these days, and the novelty had worn off with only the boredom remaining. But he was learning how to turn the boredom to his advantage; he could convert it into a kind of anger, and spread it round the committee so that they all shared the desire to get on with the matter in hand speedily. If you enjoy a committee meeting, was his dictum, you are doing it wrong.

He walked down his winding staircase in what had once been the bell-tower of St Luke's, wondering if his car, left parked overnight in the street, would or would not be vandalized. Last week, some hand, which had in his opinion to be masculine and under fifteen, possibly half of that, had scratched on it several phallic symbols. They might have been cacti or bananas but he thought not.

He could hear voices from the hall where his entrance adjoined that of Stella Pinero in St Luke's Mansions.

A light silvery voice was saying: 'They didn't worry about where the lavatories were in the Globe.'

Stella Pinero could be heard loud and clear, her voice rarely failed to hit its mark: 'I don't think they had lavatories in the Globe: they just used the back wall.'

They were standing in the hall, Stella in brown trousers and a cream shirt with a blue scarf tied round her hair. With her was what could only be their new neighbour: a tall, grey-haired man in a suede jacket as pale as his hair. He too wore a blue scarf, but his was knotted round his neck over his matching shirt. He looked distinguished. Was distinguished, since Coffin recognised him as a famous photographer.

Stella turned round.

'Oh, you've got Tiddles.'

'Have I?' He looked. He had. Tiddles had come down the stairs behind him, and was now discreetly emptying himself out of the room in the way cats have.

'You know Sir Harry, don't you?'

'By reputation.' He held out his hand. Harry Beauchamp, recently knighted, was famous for his photographic portraits and revealing group and street scenes. He had an eye. Younger than Cecil Beaton and older than Snowdon, he looked set to beat them all.

'And I know you,' said Sir Harry, giving him a tight, hard shake. 'Saw you in court when Edith Martiner came up for trial. She did it, of course.'

'Oh yes. She was lucky to get off.'

'I was doing a series of photos of different types of women. She was a type all right. Wouldn't have liked to be shut up in a room with her. Thought she'd eat me as it was. Wonder what's happened to her.'

Coffin, who knew, said nothing.

'I heard she went to Tibet, beat up a soldier and got shot.'

It was not quite the story Coffin knew, but it might have been truer than the version he had. There were so many ways of telling the truth.

'I'd be surprised if she's dead...I thought you were our new neighbour,' he said.

'Dick? I'm going to share with him. You're getting us both.'

Over his head, although tall Sir Harry was shorter than she was, he met Stella's amused, informed smile. Always do, always have, her lips breathed: a two-some.

'Sir Harry's going to do some photographs of our Work in Progress. One of the Sunday supplements is taking it. Lovely publicity for us.'

'Take some of you, if you like,' offered Sir Harry. 'Got any good crimes going? I like a bit of background material.'

There was a screech of brakes and an angry shout from outside.

'That's Tiddles crossing the road against the lights,' said Stella with resignation. 'He will do it.'

As Coffin got in his car, he saw a middle-aged man and woman standing on the pavement. He knew the woman's face, he thought she worked in the theatre for Stella. He thought they were studying him, but he did not hear what they said.

'Is that him?' asked the man.

'Yes. He's late to work today. Very punctual as a rule.'

'He looks that sort.'

'You won't—' she hesitated '—do anything, will you, Fred?'

'No. I just wanted to see him. Get to know his face.'

'How can that help, Fred? How can it help Anny?'

'It helps me,' said Fred Kinver. He strode forward, feet heavy and fast on the ground, he had always been a mover, played football in his youth in the days when there were such things as wingers and a man had to be able to run. She had a job keeping up with him.

'Walk on,' he commanded.

'They're doing what they can, Fred.'

'Doesn't it matter to you that the police haven't got the man that killed your daughter yet? It matters to me. I screamed when they told me.'

'I heard you,' said Mrs Kinver. 'You kept it up.'

'You just sat there quiet.'

'Everyone grieves differently.'

'I'm not grieving. Not just grieving. I'm working at it. That's why I wanted to see his face. You can get at that one. Get through to him. I feel better now I've seen that. I shan't let him alone.'

'Walk on.'

They walked on. Beyond St Luke's Mansions where Coffin lived and the theatre was rising, past the new police building, down the slope of Feather Street where the Zemans and the Annecks and the Darbyshires lived and where the small dairy, home to Jim Marsh and his father, clung to the bottom of the slope.

'That's where he lives,' whispered Mrs Kinver, 'the boy who found Anny.'

'That tart's son,' said Fred Kinver mechanically. He strode on.

I am vengeance, thought Fred Kinver, and I will have my way.

Jim Marsh looking down from his high window saw the two of them and picked up what Fred Kinver was feeling. Something about the hunch of Fred's shoulder and the way his head was thrust forward. Vengeance personified, he thought, and his own imagination caught fire.

# TWO

*Tuesday morning through to evening, May 30, to Wednesday, May 31*

FIVE, NEARLY SIX DAYS after the finding of the body in Rope Alley felt like three months in Leathergate and the neighbouring area of Spinnergate, for unease spread over here too. Murderers came from anywhere, this one could be far away by now, but he could be local. Was most likely local, everyone said, because of knowing about Rope Alley, dark even in sunlight and with several hiding places in it as well as a quick exit at each end.

'I THINK IT'S as bad about the boy as anything I've ever heard. I mean...him finding her. After his mother.' The elder Mrs Zeman spoke to her niece. They were sitting over the tea-table, Mrs Zeman favoured a strong blend of Darjeeling, procured at her own special shop in Brook Street. She sipped her tea which was piping hot, just how she liked it. 'His mother,' she repeated, between sips. 'It must have reminded him.'

'She killed herself, Aunt Kay.'

Her niece had her own small pot of Earl Grey; as with so much of their life together there were carefully defined boundaries. Tea was one of them. Coffee, decaffeinated or not, was another.

Aunt Kay Zeman sniffed. 'She always was unreliable.'

'She managed that all right.'

Mrs Zeman did not relent. 'I've always thought it was an accident.'

'And he didn't find her. No one did.'

Not for several months anyway, until the river finally delivered her on a muddy bank down the estuary. But of course they knew where she'd gone and where she'd gone in: she left plenty of evidence around. It had never been Clare Marsh's idea not to punish someone. The only thing was, reflected the niece, she had punished plenty of people who didn't deserve it.

'Not entirely the husband's fault,' said Mrs Zeman judicially.

'I should think not indeed.'

'All the same, he's trouble. Not really suitable to be your lover.'

'He's not my lover.'

It was Mrs Zeman's idea that her niece did have a lover somewhere, but she had not so far been able to get positive proof of the victim's identity although she had her ideas. She thought of him as a victim. In her experience, lovers were victims, as well as victors, torments, and objects of delight.

She said no more, contenting herself with this probe. Her niece, child of her younger sister, long dead, was called Valerie, which Mrs Zeman regarded as an awkward, unlucky name. Valerie had certainly been some witness to the truth of this belief since she had been a failure as an artist (she had a wooden studio in Aunt Kay's garden, rent: looking after her aunt), and as a woman with a string of abandoned relationships behind her.

'You must try and attract someone, Val, hold on, instead of being always a failure.'

'A lucky failure,' she retorted at once to this probing sally of Aunt Kay's, 'because I've ended up happier than you by a long shot.'

Katherine Zeman did not believe this: in her eyes no woman was happy without a settled marriage and at least one son.

'Happiness is not what an adult expects,' she replied. 'A woman should hold on to her man. I held on to mine. You did not. You are a bad chooser.'

'Someone will kill you one day, Aunt Kay,' said Val, 'and it just might be me.'

Mrs Zeman poured another cup of tea. Milk first, she always said, otherwise it stains the cups. Her son had told her that her tea, dark and strong, had long since stained her gullet and stomach deep brown. She did not believe him. Her body would naturally not allow such liberties. She and Val, both strong characters, enjoyed, in fact, a happy relationship in which their sharp differences of opinion were not only allowed but pleasurable. Each knew the frontiers over which not to step and if Mrs Zeman sometimes, as now, strayed too far over them, then she felt it allowed to her as an old woman. It was one of the taxes she levied on Val's good humour, part of her rent.

'The girl wasn't one of Leonard's patients, was she?'

Valerie occasionally acted as Dr Leonard Zeman's receptionist and secretary, keeping his records in her fine clear handwriting, so she knew who was on his list.

'No, I believe she's with the Elmgate practice.' The Elmgate Health Centre was a large group of some six doctors near to the Spinnergate Tube station, and was popular with all the company at the St Luke's Workshop theatre. Dr Greer was the company physician. 'But Tim knew her, of course.'

'Sweet on her, was he?'

'I don't know, Auntie. She was very pretty.'

'Wouldn't be surprised, then.' In fact, surprised if not. Tim Zeman had an eye for the girls, thought his grandmother complacently. She knew less about Tim than Val did. 'Well, he wasn't with us that day.'

'No, Auntie.' In fact, they hadn't seen him for some time. Old Mrs Zeman minded, although she hated to admit it. 'I believe he was with some friends in Kent.' The young Edens, Angus Eden had been at school with Tim. He had an even younger and prettier wife.

'Have you seen him since?'

'No, he's been keeping himself to himself.'

'Upset, I expect.'

'I think he's just working for his exams, Aunt Kay.'

'Certainly what he ought to be doing. Pour some more tea, dear.'

Another cup of dark liquid went down to join the buttered tea-bun and the toasted tea-cake. Yet she was not fat, as Valerie, who put on weight quickly, noticed and thought unfair.

'Anyway, it's not Tim, I'm worried about.'

'I didn't know you were worried.'

'I am always worried.'

'All right. Who especially this time?'

'I'm worried about Leonard.'

Val drank some tea. 'Why Leonard?'

'I don't think he is happy. And I am sure that Felicity is not.'

'Well, it's probably her job. Always dealing with sick babies. It's a wounding profession.'

'She cures them.'

'Sometimes, but not always. Not often, probably. She gets all the serious cases.'

'It's her marriage. Something wrong there. I feel it.'

Valerie shrugged. If Aunt Kay Zeman felt it, then she would go on feeling it, and nothing would shake her.

'Do you think she's got a lover?'

'Really, Aunt Kay, I don't know.'

'And wouldn't say if you did know,' said Mrs Zeman in a not unamiable way. 'I like loyalty in a woman.'

Val shrugged. So did she, but it was a hard commodity to come by. 'Sex isn't always the trouble.'

'It mostly is. Think of that poor girl. Sex killed her.'

'All right. I suppose it did. Being the wrong sex.' Boys got killed too, of course, but not so often. Not nearly so often. And hardly ever by girls, usually by a member of their own sex.

'So what do you think is the trouble with Leonard?'

She wasn't going to give up, this was developing into what the family called 'searching sessions'. Search being the operative word.

'Do you think he's got a lover?'

'Why don't you ask him?'

'I did, and he just laughed. His father wouldn't have laughed. I didn't know what to make of it.'

'I expect the answer is No, then,' said Val, 'and he just didn't want to disappoint you.'

'He's very in with that theatre crowd,' said Mrs Zeman broodingly. 'And so are you. Get me tickets for their next production, will you? I don't trust that Pinero woman. Got a roving eye.'

'Oh, Aunt Kay,' said Val. 'People don't talk that way any more.'

'They act that way, though,' retorted Katherine Zeman with grim pleasure.

Val took the two tea-trays through into the kitchen. Her tray with the china pot of Earl Grey tea from Fortnum's and the thin coconut biscuits from the same shop, and Mrs Zeman's large silver teapot of the best Darjeeling with the covered dish of hot tea-buns. They occasionally raided each other's supply of eatables (there was a rich chocolate biscuit cake which they both liked) but never the teapots.

Through the open kitchen door Val could see down their garden to the garden across the way. The Annecks, that would be. Their lilac tree was in full bloom, a pleasure to behold, but in return the Zeman roses would presently be scenting the air for the Annecks.

On the skyline she could see the tower of St Luke's old church, now called St Luke's Mansions, where dwelt, among others, her friend Stella Pinero whose reputation she had just defended. There was a small Theatre Club in Feather Street of which she was secretary; all of them were Friends of the St Luke's Theatre and got special rates for a season's subscription.

She poured a bowl of tea and milk for Bob, the black and white dog; he liked Darjeeling, liked it weak and lukewarm. Now he tongued it up with great slurping noises, he was not a neat dog.

The telephone rang on the wall in the kitchen. All callers were well aware that Kay Zeman, wherever she was in the house, might grab an extension.

Val lifted the receiver. No, she couldn't hear Aunt Kay's breathing, but that didn't mean she wasn't there.

'Hello?'

'Leonard here. I want to talk. Is it all right?'

He meant who's with you.

'I'm in the kitchen on my own,' said Val with caution.

'The police have been questioning Tim about the Kinver girl. Her murder, that is. Asking how well he knew her, where he was that day and so on.'

Where had he been, Val wondered. 'I expect they are going round all the girl's friends,' she said.

'So I suppose.'

'Who told you?'

'Not Tim,' said his father with feeling. 'Mrs Anneck rang up. They had Peter in.'

'Well, there you are then. The police are just doing the rounds.'

'Don't tell Mother. I don't want her worried, her heart's bad.'

Val sighed. 'She'll pick it up. She's sending out signals like a TV station as it is. She might very well be listening now.'

'About the murder?'

'Not only that. She wonders if you have a lover.' She held the receiver to her ear, listening carefully.

Leonard Zeman managed a laugh; he too had heard the sound of breathing. Mother had arrived. Where had she been until now? Probably cleaning her teeth after all that strong tea.

'Or if Felicity has one, or even me. But she thinks I'm a failure there.' Val did not mind repeating this; after all, it was no news to Mrs Zeman, whose breathing could be clearly heard now, and Leonard ought to know.

'Tell her I'm sending her medicine round, will you? It's a new tablet prescribed for her to try.' Not by him, of course, but by one of his partners, he did not treat his own family. 'See she takes the proper dose, will you?'

The conversation moved on to things medical which it was perfectly allowable for Mrs Zeman to overhear, and which, indeed, he was talking about so that she could.

He and Val had learnt plenty of tricks.

As she leant against the kitchen wall talking, Val could see Mary Anneck come out of her back door and walk down the garden path with her dog.

MRS ANNECK strolled down the paved way between the geraniums with her Jack Russell nipping at her heels. She was used to this, wore stout shoes and boots sometimes on purpose.

She knew she was right to have telephoned Leonard Zeman. She had the feeling that at a time like this they must stick together. The police had been in her house interviewing her older son, Peter, her daughter, her daughter's current boyfriend (although he hadn't been that last week and might not be next, they changed so fast), and her young son Adrian. She supposed that they had to question all Anna's friends, although it was hardly likely Adrian could be of much use to them since he was only twelve, but you never knew these days.

It was what you never knew that made her heart sink.

'Be quiet, Edie,' she said to the terrier bitch who had caught sight, or thought she had, of a whisker of her brother and best enemy through the garden hedge and was screaming in fury.

Mary Anneck concluded that the dogs would get no regular exercise until the dog-walker, Jim Marsh, had recovered his balance. He must be having quite a time with the police too, poor boy.

Like Kay Zeman she was worried about him. Life could be so unfair. She thought he'd had enough. He always looked so frail physically too, with those narrow bones and that thin face, but of course, he couldn't be, because he walked all the dogs and handled them beautifully. She must try and feed him up, she was a great believer in red meat and none of this vegetarian business that his mother Clare had gone in for. Anorexic she'd been in Mary's opinion and her death no disaster to anyone once they'd got over the shock.

It was a mystery why Clare had killed herself, but by all account she'd made one or two earlier attempts. Perhaps she just didn't like being a milkman's wife. And that was no joke, thought Mary Anneck, because Clare had almost certainly started out life with different ideas. Philosophy at Oxford, hadn't it been?

Then to her surprise, she heard the bell ringing from the Darbyshires' back door, which must mean that Jumbo (their little disaster of a dog was called Jumbo, although he was the smallest, shortest Jack Russell imaginable) was going out on his walk. And since Philippa Darbyshire had broken her ankle, and her Harold hated the dog even more than Jumbo hated him, it must mean that Jim Marsh was on the job. With any luck he would come for Edie next.

PHILIPPA DARBYSHIRE limped back to her chair from her bell-ringing exercise, thankful to see the back of Jumbo for a bit. With plenty of exercise you could just be in the same room with him; without a lot he was unbearable. He was always unbearable, Harold said, but that was unkind. Jumbo had defended Philippa from a mugger once, and although it had been a task after his own heart, and the mugger had felt desexed by his wounds for some months and had considered claiming damages, it had ensured Jumbo a longer life than might otherwise have been expected, taking his ferocious habits into account.

Philippa herself was still shaken from the death of Anna Mary. Since no payment was asked she had tutored the girl in extra mathematics for her computer studies out of love of the subject and sympathy with the girl, so ambitious, so pretty, so badly taught elsewhere. Harold had helped here too.

She had been questioned by the police and so too had Harold. She hadn't liked the idea of that interrogation, because that was what it had been judging by Harold's face afterwards, cross and white. What had Harold got to do with the death of this girl he hardly knew? He only saw her when she came to the house for tutorials.

The boys would be back from Scotland tomorrow, when no doubt the police would want to interview them too. They had been friendly enough with Anna, close even, she knew it and no doubt that smooth policeman Inspector Young knew it too. They had not been in London the night she was killed. Presumably you called that an alibi.

She might have a talk with Valerie Humberstone about it, Val was about her closest friend, but she thought that Val had troubles of her own.

Stella Pinero could be more helpful, she knew how to give advice. Had been through the mill herself. Many a time and oft, as she had once said with feeling. Stella was not a close friend, but an admired one, and the girl's mother had worked for her. Still did, probably, if she was up to working for anyone now. Mrs Kinver had worked for Philippa herself once, but when the offer of a job at the theatre had come up, she had been unable to resist it. Philippa had understood, she was stage-struck herself.

It was a horrible business, but the police would soon sort it out.

On this hopeful note, she awaited the arrival of Jim Marsh to exercise old Jumbo.

TWO DAYS, three days, a week. Unease was still oiling itself all over Leathergate with Spinnergate feeling it too. The discomfort, quite physical for some people like the Kinvers, husband and wife, reached even St Luke's Theatre Workshop where the company directed by Stella Pinero had embarked on advance preparation for its most ambitious production so far.

They needed something popular so they were going to do *Cavalcade*, using local actors for part of the huge cast. Not that their cast was going to be Drury Lane big. Stella had pruned sternly.

Using local talent was a wise political gesture (low cunning some said) since the theatre received a grant on condition it hired graduates from the Drama De-

partment of the new Dockside University. Using am-
ateurs fulfilled the spirit of the thing, Stella
maintained, with the advantage they did not have to
be paid. She was always short of ready cash. Lætitia
Bingham, her ultimate controller, kept them on a
rolling budget.

Hopefuls were flooding in for audition, their arri-
vals organized by several amateur acting societies and
the Theatre Club in which Mary Anneck and Philippa Darbyshire were prominent. But with this flood
came also a spate of rumours and anxieties about the
murder of Anna Mary.

She was surprised how guilty many felt. Guilt and
alarm seemed spread about the community. Somehow it was their fault, they were a bad lot in Leathergate and getting no better.

John Coffin came in for a drink that evening, one
full week after the discovery of Anna Mary's body in
Rope Walk, bringing Tiddles with him. Tiddles liked
a sweet sherry in a saucer.

'Any news?' She stirred a cocktail, she was learning to make them now, they were the smart thing, and
anyway she wanted to get into the Coward mood.

'Don't make that thing too sweet, will you?' Coffin stared at what she was doing disapprovingly. 'I
can't bear sweet drinks. About the murder? No,
nothing much.'

'This brew will be as bitter as hell.' Stella handed
over the drink.

He had seen all the usual reports, of course, forensic, technical, photographic, made a point of it, so his
comment was not strictly true, but there was no news
that counted. Not what she meant. No strong suspect
in sight.

'I miss Mrs Kinver. She came in to work today, but she wasn't really with us, I sent her back home.'

'She might have been better working.'

'I thought of that, of course, but her husband turned up, was walking up and down outside, frightened to let her out of his sight. That worried her. Worried me, too. He's in a bad way, John, taking it worse than the mother, really, although you can never be sure what's going on inside.'

Coffin frowned and sipped his drink. Repulsive, he thought, and looked for somewhere to pour it away. 'He needs help. I can probably get him some. We have a psychiatrist on the Force who specializes in helping victims of violence.'

'Is he good?'

'I think so. He helped me.'

Stella gave Coffin a surprised look, but he did not explain his words.

'I think Kinver'd like to kill someone,' she said. 'Anyone, but preferably the murderer of his girl.'

'Is that what his wife thinks?'

'I bet it is.'

'Then she needs help too.'

The telephone rang.

He managed to slip his drink into Tiddle's saucer while Stella's attention was diverted. Tiddles took a sip, then looked at him with a baleful green stare. Poisoning me, are you? the stare said. Well, I know what to do about that. Tiddles stepped in the saucer, overturning it.

She turned round from her desk. 'It's for you. How did they know where to find you?'

He shrugged. 'They always know where I am.'

He took the telephone. His old friend Superintendent Paul Lane passing on a report from Archie Young. He listened. 'Yes, that is interesting. Good. Keep me up to date.'

He returned to Stella. 'Swinehouse have picked up a man with dried blood on his clothes. And a knife.'

Stella stared. 'Wouldn't he change his clothes? If he was the killer?'

'Yes. If he could. This man could not. He couldn't, didn't have any.'

A vagrant. Living rough.

NEXT DAY WAS the day on which they had the first letter from the Paper Man.

It was sent straight to John Coffin himself, as if the writer wanted to be sure he got it.

# THREE

WHEN THEY PARTED that evening, John Coffin to see an exhibition of designs of uniforms for his new Force and Stella to make a speech at a Charity dinner about 'Theatre in the New City', in a reversal of their usual roles, she said to him fiercely:

'Go and see this man they've detained. Go yourself. Don't feed me that stuff about it not being your job any more. It's all your job. Take a look yourself. The Kinvers deserve that you should.'

'Would you like me to make your speech for you?' he observed mildly. 'Then you can do my job and choose the uniforms.'

'Do what I ask. You always do what I ask.'

'Not always.'

'Oh, come on, you love me.'

'Like a brother.'

'I have heard of incest,' she said hopefully.

'Times have changed.'

'It's not times, it's people.' She put on her sad face and walked to the window, carrying Tiddles and her cocktail glass.

Beautifully done, he thought. 'Shall I clap?'

'Pig.'

'I'll see the man.'

'Not so changed, then.'

'I was going to anyway, you're not the only one with a personal interest.' He hadn't known the girl, nor her parents, but a long while ago he had been involved in a series of similar murders of women, and the scar of that terrible case remained.*

Stella, who had known him in those days, and nearly been a victim herself, nodded. 'We go a long way back, you and I. Go and select your uniforms. I'll be here when you come back. If you choose, that is.'

Outside the door, he leant hard on it so that Tiddles could not follow. 'I'm learning. How many years, and I'm learning at last.'

THE MAN IN the cell had been reluctant to change his bloodsoaked clothes for the fresh ones provided by the police. They didn't fit, he said, too long in the arm and short in the leg.

'I'm not a bloody gorilla.'

He had been in police hands for over twenty-four hours when Coffin saw him and in that time had said little else. But he had been picked up wearing bloodstained clothes and carrying a knife of the kind which could have slashed Anna Mary Kinver.

Forensic tests were now going on to determine if the blood was hers. (No wound on the man, who would not give his name, so the blood was not his.) The knife too was being examined.

A witness claimed to have seen a man like him hanging about in the neighbourhood of Rope Alley for some hours on the day of the murder.

As Coffin arrived an identity parade was just about to take place. Not to his surprise, an old friend, Mim-

* *Coffin on the Water*

sie Marker, who sold newspapers outside Spinnergate
Tube Station, was the witness. She was known as the
eyes and ears of Leathergate, Spinnergate, East Spinnergate and Easthythe. The district of Swinehouse was
just a bit too far away even for her excellent sensory
perceptions. People had been known to move there,
just to get away from Mimsie. But those were her en-
emies, most people admired Mimsie. Liking was
harder. Coffin was one of those who managed both.

Mimsie went slowly down the line. She took her
time. It was not her first exploit of this sort and she
knew the ropes.

'A job lot, you've got here,' she said in a judicial
manner. 'I wouldn't say you matched them up any too
well. Still, there's not many like him. That's him.' She
nodded. 'Number Seven.'

Number Seven, who had not wanted to be number
seven, protesting that it was an unlucky number, was
a tall, thin man with a face that looked as if the dirt
had worked in over the years and would now never
wash out. It was probably the case, Coffin thought.

The line-up of men were returned to their own lives,
and No. 7 back to his cell.

'There all day, he was,' declared Mimsie. She gave
John Coffin a nod as from one old friend to another,
both equal, which they certainly were, and more since
Mimsie was reputed to keep a sock of gold under her
bed.

'All day, Mimsie?' asked Detective-Inspector
Young, who knew his Mimsie.

'Perhaps not all day, not every bloody hour, what
do you expect, he's only human whatever he looks
like. Most of the day. On and off. He did move around
a bit. But he was there.'

'You'll go into court and say so?'

'Of course.'

'Thanks, Mimsie.'

After she had gone, he said to Coffin. 'She's a good witness, goes into court like a soldier.'

'Have you got anything else besides Mimsie putting him in the place at the right time?'

Archie Young shook his head. 'Waiting for forensics.'

'Anything from the man? Identity, past record?'

'He hasn't got a record,' said Young regretfully. 'As far as we know, he is baby-clean.'

'What about Interpol?'

Young gave his chief a sharp look. 'He has got a foreign look, I picked that up too, but I think it's just dirt. His clothes seem to be English. But we are trying Amsterdam.' He considered it for a moment. 'I dare say they won't know him, he looks nameless to me. You get an instinct about these things, and that's how I feel about him.'

No. 7, when brought in for questioning, elected to remain silent. He did not deny being in Rope Alley nor admit it, but just let the questions wash over him like the water to which he seemed so alien.

He was a man whose eyes roamed round the room all the time, but never resting on a face. Narrow brown eyes with large violet stains beneath them. Still quite a young man, he had plenty of hair and his teeth were white, not broken or jagged. His hands were the worst thing about him, worse even than the perpetually moving eyes; they were long-fingered with chewed nails and scarred and stained. The wrists had their own set of scars, some dark red and new, others old and puckered as if these parts of him had led a battered life of their own.

Somewhere some mental hospital must have known him, possibly even now some anxious social worker was wondering where he was, speculated Coffin. But possibly not, he looked like a man who would manage everything on his own, even his own death. It might be very hard to track his passage through the world.

While Coffin studied him, he started to walk about the interview room with big, fast steps. Young sprang to his feet.

'Leave him,' said Coffin.

No. 7 paced up and down the room.

Finally, as he was led away, he said: 'Of course, I did it, but you'll never prove it.'

'Won't we, by God,' said Young. 'If he did it, then we will prove it.'

'But you don't think he did?'

Archie Young was silent. Then he gave a shrug. 'Doesn't look so good somehow. I'm beginning to think not. The forensics will help. Maybe decide.'

'I don't think so, either,' said Coffin. 'I think he's just having a bit of fun at our expense.' But he didn't look like a character with a whole lot of fun in him.

'Heartless as a shark,' said Young.

'What else have you got going?'

'I'm still working on the girl's friends. Looking into the lot. Every one she knew. Kids at the disco she went to every week. Even her father.'

'There's something else. Don't know what to make of it yet.'

He went to his desk, removed a manilla folder from a drawer and handed it over to Coffin.

'I went over her room at home. Found these tucked away under a pile of tights.'

A roll of writing paper. Three pages. Each page had faint typewritten lines on it.

What he had before him were three short poems. He read them with a frown.

'Love poems,' he said aloud. 'Faintly pornographic, but fairly harmless.'

'Shows something,' said Archie Young. 'Shows something about her. Don't know what yet, but I hope to find out. Don't know who wrote them to her either, but I'll find that out too.'

'Any idea?'

'I'm thinking of the people in Feather Street,' he said. 'They're an educated lot. I showed these poems to my wife. She writes poetry. She says they are good poems. In their way. Not what she'd write, but good.'

The Zemans, the Annecks and the Darbyshires were the names in his mind.

'The poems may not have anything to do with her murder, of course,' said Coffin.

But he agreed it was something to work on.


WHEN COFFIN got home, he found the letter from the Paper Man waiting for him.

The letter was correctly addressed to him.

Chief Commander John Coffin, OBE. And the right address in St Luke's Mansions. He had been accurately researched.

The communication was built up of letters cut out of newspapers and magazines, a kind of job lot, all sizes and colours and shapes.

The message was short:

*The man you have in custody is not the right one. If you don't get the right one, I will do the job for you.*

This letter had no address, not to be expected, and no signature. The name Paper Man came later.

THE POLICE WERE still optimistic of an early conclusion to their investigation.

No. 7 was still on their books, not entirely in the clear, far from it, he kept saying he had done it, and he had described her killing. He had seen it, if nothing else. But the blood on his jacket was animal blood, source unknown, while the knife could not have been the weapon: the blade was the wrong shape. Nor did his body secretions match those found on Anna's body.

They had the poems. They were looking for the silver shoe. They were still hopeful.

But as time went on, it all went cold on them.

# FOUR

*The days of Friday to Wednesday, June 2 to 7.*

FRED KINVER WAS building his own paper palace at home in Elder Street. He had collected all the newspaper reports of the killing of his daughter which he had stuck on a board in the kitchen. They lived for most of the time in the kitchen, so they were under his eyes as he ate and worked. The distress they caused his wife was ignored by him. Two sturdy piles of newspapers with their coloured supplements stood on a table by the door. On them was a handwritten sign: NOT TO TOUCH.

She did not touch. Wouldn't have dreamt of it. She turned her eyes aside every time she went past.

Nearly two weeks after the killing, with the police investigation stuck, these reports were naturally less frequent, but Fred Kinver was pursuing his research in other channels.

'Just off,' he called to his wife who was making the bed upstairs. 'I've washed the breakfast things.' Not quite true, he had held them under the tap and left them on the side to drain, tea stains and marmalade marked them still, his wife would have to do them again. But she was prepared for this, and did so every day. The thing is to keep him occupied, she told herself, and not to let him know he does not do things well.

'Where are you going?' She didn't really like him out of her sight just now. He had to protect her. She had to protect him.

'The library.' Not quite true on this point either, as he had another call to make in addition. 'Don't forget to take your tablets the doctor gave you.' He usually said this as he left.

'The library's not open yet,' she muttered to herself. 'Won't be for another hour.' Did he think she was a fool? The answer was that he did, and didn't like questions, either.

She heard the front door go and then a click.

'He's locked me in.' She sighed. The back door would be locked as well, and all the keys gone. He was doing it a lot lately. And not by accident, either. She would have to get herself another set of keys cut or life would be even more difficult for her than it was at present. She grieved deeply for her daughter, but she had hung on to rationality. It didn't look as though Fred had.

Fred Kinver walked briskly to his small allotment hard by the former Brazen Head Dock, now changing into a hotel and leisure centre. His allotment might be swallowed up by their tennis courts but at the moment Fred and about a dozen others were still in possession.

Here Fred had the wooden hut that he called his 'office'. He did keep a few papers, old bills and diaries here. Otherwise he used it for a smoke, a quiet drink, and talk with a few old friends. It was locked, or appeared to be so, but the padlock had long since been broken and hung there for show. All Fred's friends knew you could get in if you wanted.

When Fred went there, as he did often, no one noticed him because he was a familiar figure. He had
looked the same for years, grey-haired, spectacled, of
medium height, and on the thin side. Winter or summer he wore the same old tweed jacket and raincoat.
By the same token, he did not notice much about others. Jim Marsh, riding past on his father's milk-float,
saw Fred going across to his allotment. His father had
told him to keep away from Fred because of family
reasons, which prohibition he obeyed without meaning to keep for ever. He didn't like Fred.

Now Fred went into his 'office' and sat down for
work. He was keeping a kind of diary. Perhaps not a
diary, more an account of a life.

After he had filled in a few paragraphs, he rose and
hid it in a corner of the hut, under a box of lettuce
seedlings that he would probably now never plant out.
They were already yellow and sorry-looking. Casualties of the war he was fighting.

Then he went on to what he called his next appointment. At the Library.

The new Spinnergate District Library in Puddle
Lane was a long, low building put together from the
dark red brick so popular locally. It replaced an Ed-
wardian building of stern construction which had re-
sisted bombs in two world wars and very nearly
defeated the 1980's demolition team.

The old building had been a comfortable home for
books, mice and men. The new one, although light
and warm, seemed less welcoming somehow, and
mysteriously appeared to have fewer books. The li-
brarians explained this by saying that there were just
as many books, but they just looked fewer on the new
shelving. Hardly anyone believed them and Fred, a

regular attender and borrower since his unemployment set in like a long illness from which he would never recover, was able to name several of his favourite books that had definitely disappeared. *The Giant Book of Mysteries*, for one. Also *The Boy's Book of Sea Stories*, an old favourite which had gone from the 'Books for Younger Readers' shelves.

He made for the reference library, which was quiet and well stocked with files of newspapers going back over the last decade. The Spinnergate Library was a library of reference for South Docklands. It was much used by the Sixth Form College down the road and occasionally by students from the University. The room was never empty, but there was a live and let live feeling about the place: you kept quiet and did not interfere with the other readers.

This was just as well since they had been seen doing rather odd things. Eating was not allowed in the library, but there was no doubt that old Mr. Rough had been noticed chewing a piece of cold toast. A late breakfast, he had maintained. Mrs Armitage knitted a dark blue sock which never seemed to get finished; she must unravel it in the night like one of those strange Nordic goddesses, and would ask to measure it against your foot if you would be so kind, which was harmless enough but not what the Library was meant for. Two female students had been seen holding hands in one corner and one of them, weeping, had run out before anything could be said to them.

Fred Kinver went into the stacks behind the main library where the files of newspapers, both local and national, were kept in great bound volumes.

He was systematically going through them collecting material on John Coffin. Personal details of the man's life (not many of those, he had not been free with information about himself to the Press), photographs, and anything that came to hand about the cases he had worked on. Over the years Coffin had had a fair amount of publicity, so Fred had a harvest. When the new Force was created and John Coffin appointed he had figured in several major articles in *The Times* and the *Independent*.

As soon as he came across anything that interested him, Fred took out a tiny knife and quietly cut it out. No one saw. He did a bit every day, never too much, but taking his mite of paper daily, like a rodent.

He smiled as he did so.

When he got home the day's haul would be pasted neatly in a big scrapbook, which he planned to take round to his 'office' as soon as it was up to date. He was reluctant to do this, as he would rather have had it to hand, but in the end, if left in the house, his wife would find it. She found everything.

'Valuable archive information,' he muttered as he stowed away today's bag, and then went off to choose a new book to take out.

'You're doing a lot of reading lately, Mr Kinver,' said the cheeky girl at the desk as she fed his tickets into her machine.

He did not answer.

Stiff-necked old thing, thought the girl. 'No manners,' she complained to her colleague.

'Don't think he heard you.'

'What's more, I think he always takes the same book out.'

'Oh, he's one of those, is he?'

They had several like that.

On his way home Fred loaded up with all the daily papers that Mimsie Marker had left on her stall by the Tube station. She let him have them cheaply in a bundle. She was sorry for him.

'It's not good for you to keep reading everything about Anna, but I can see why you feel you must,' she said.

'Do you?' In a way she probably did, but not entirely. 'I'm collecting information.' He didn't mind talking to her: she was old Spinnergate village, not like the red-faced little girl in the Library, an alien if ever he saw one.

'The police are better at that, Fred.'

'Are they?' He leaned forward and looked her in the eye. The one eye that really looked at you, the other wandered. 'But do they draw the right conclusions?'

He was angry, but it seemed more than that, Mimsie thought. 'So what are all the newspapers for?' She didn't know about what he did in the Library, but from the way she spoke she might almost have guessed it.

'Background material.'

There wasn't much of that, she thought, but he was obsessed.

'Fourteen days, that's three hundred and thirty-six hours, and I don't know how many minutes since Anna was killed, and they still haven't got the man.'

'It's early days.'

'And it's staring them in the face,' said Fred Kinver. 'I'll set things right.'

Mimsie said: 'Fred, we've been chums a long time, haven't we? You can trust me. You're not up to something, are you?'

But he didn't trust anyone then, not Mimsie, not his wife, not John Coffin, no one except himself could set things right. For it was not just information he was collecting, he was somehow fuelling himself up for what he meant to do.

A naturally timid and peaceful man, more fitted for making biscuits than taking action, he needed strength.

'It's quite clear who killed her,' he said. 'Why don't they listen to what Anna said. I listen all the time.'

He strode off.

'You've left your change,' Mimsie called after him, but he did not hear.

She could see he was not taking the road home to Elder Street. He was turning left. Wherever he was going, that way was not home.

Now what was that way, she asked herself?

Nearly everything that counted in Spinnergate. The University, the two big scholars, St Peter's Hospital, St Luke's Mansion and theatre complex, the new police headquarters and the river.

Not the river, she hoped.

OH, NOT THE RIVER, thought Elsie Kinver, still in her prison. She would have to break a window if she wanted to get out, yet she would do that if she got desperate enough. The shepherd's pie was in the oven and he hadn't come home to eat it, so that it was pale brown and dry now. Neither of them had much appetite at the moment, but you had to try. 'He wouldn't do that to me. He knows I couldn't stand to lose both of them.'

She knew a little more about her daughter than Fred did, because she made the beds and did the housework and she had found the sexy poems long before the police.

Not mentioned them to Anna Mary, though. The girl had a right to her own life.

She hadn't been shocked. 'Wouldn't have minded some poems like that myself when I was her age. Fat chance from Fred.'

Naturally she hadn't mentioned them to Fred, hoped he didn't know. Goodness knows what he would have done if he'd found them. It didn't bear thinking about.

The police had them in their possession now, of course, but as far as she knew, they had not told Fred.

Where was he now, and what was he up to?

What was he up to?

JOHN COFFIN looked down on the river from his office window. He couldn't see it from where he lived in St Luke's Mansions, so this was a bonus. He was fond of the Thames which had been part of his life. He could just remember when it had been filled with merchant shipping, now it was empty except for a few small vessels which moored at the Brazen Head Dock from time to time. All the big carriers had moved down to the estuary where the water was deeper. The romantic upper Thames, north of Oxford, so beloved of poets and scholars, had little appeal for him whose river was the London river, the tidal river of docks and working craft.

An uproar in his outer office drew him back from the window. Such noise did not usually disturb the Head of the Force. He was a sacred object to be treated with respect. A boring fact, but true.

What were they having, a riot?

But no, it was just one man's voice, shouting, and his secretary shouting back. He was surprised she could shout, she never raised her voice with him.

Someone banged against his door, collided with it, and then opened it. He saw a dishevelled middle-aged man with grey hair and frantic eyes. But he looked determined.

No gun that Coffin could see, so he probably was not dangerous. He could hear bells sounding in the distance and knew that help would be rushing in. Still, the man should not have got through every barrier.

He recognized Fred Kinver at once, but he did not say so. Instead, he stood there waiting. Always let the other fellow plunge in.

'Got you,' said Fred Kinver. 'It's you I want.'

Coffin still waited.

'It's about the murder of my girl, my Anna. I'm Fred Kinver. I know who killed her.'

Coffin looked across to his secretary. 'It's all right, Edith. Calm everything down, will you? Come in, Mr Kinver.'

Fred was already in, sitting himself confidentially down upon the chair facing Coffin's at the big desk. The sunlight fell on his face. It wasn't that he was a bold or pushing man, Coffin understood, but that he was out of himself at the moment. He had worked himself up to do what he must do.

'I come to you because you are the top man and my wife knows you.'

Coffin nodded. He had met Mrs Kinver in Stella's dressing-room.

'She says you're a good man. I tried the others—' your underlings, he implied '—and got no good from them. Wouldn't listen. Well, they did listen, but wouldn't hear.'

A fair enough judgement, Coffin thought, on Archie Young when feeling sure of himself.

Coffin made a sudden decision. He rose and went to the door. 'Let's have some coffee, please, Edith.' This chap was living in a world of his own, perhaps coffee would drag him out of it.

'Ten minutes,' he said. 'That's what you can have. Say what you have to say and then get out.'

As things were, it was a generous ration of his day.

'It's what she said, what Anna said. She didn't say 'Get the man who killed me.' She couldn't talk like that when she was dying. What she said was 'Get Zeman. He killed me.'

Tim Zeman. Dr and Felicity Zeman's beloved son. Timmy Zeman.

'Did you write me a letter?' asked Coffin. 'Anonymously?'

'No, certainly not. Of course not, anything I have to say I'd say to your face. I have said it: the Zeman boy killed my girl.'

He was not entirely in his right mind, thought Coffin, and who could blame him?

IN THE NEXT FEW DAYS the police poured in and out of the Zeman house.

'We'd thought of it for ourselves,' said Archie Young. 'Of course we had. Be fools not to. And we were planning to concentrate on the boy Zeman. He wrote the poems. Admits it.'

They interviewed Leonard Zeman, Felicity, his wife, and of course, Tim himself. Then they moved down the road to Mrs Kay Zeman and Val Humberstone.

Mrs Zeman took to her bed with a mild heart attack, where Val waited upon her. No good was got from either of them.

They questioned the ambulance man again, and spoke to Jim Marsh. Jim said, Yes, he had heard Anna speak, but he hadn't been close, keeping the dog away, you see, and couldn't be sure what he'd heard. He did not like being questioned, wasn't a bit happy with the attention he was getting.

Then they took Tim in for questioning.

Yes, admitted the frightened boy, he had written the poems. But he hadn't killed Anna. He had been away at the time. He could prove it. He had been staying with friends in Kent, a young married couple called Eden. They would bear him out, only at the moment they were abroad.

He was kept overnight in the clean new cell in the police station that had only been opened last year, but where the cell had acquired a smell of its own. Next morning he was collected by his mother.

She drove him away in her large Mercedes car of which Tim was simultaneously proud of her owning and ashamed at the same time. It was flashy, expensive, all the things his mother wasn't really.

They were alike, these two. Tim had his father's height and his short sight but her delicate bones and pretty features. They even looked pretty on him although he was masculine enough. Birdlike, both of them.

'I didn't do it, Mother.'

'Of course, not. You don't have to tell me.'

I'd believe you even if you had done it, she thought. Mothers always do. My son is innocent, that's what they always said, didn't they? He is a nice boy. That was the other thing they said.

'About the poems—they didn't mean anything. You understand, Mum, don't you? It was just a kind of experiment, the sort of thing you have to do.'

'Of course.' She'd said it again, she really must find a different way of expressing herself. And she was driving much too fast, she'd nearly shaved that cyclist off his wheels.

'And we never did anything much, Anna and I, if you get me. And if we had, would it have mattered?'

No, it wouldn't have mattered. Anna had not been a virgin anyway at the time of her death. Some sexual experience, the medical grapevine said, and why not? Who expected otherwise? . .

'Why didn't you get me out before? Why did I have to stay in there all night? It was foul.'

'The police had a right to question you, Tim. You aren't a minor any more.'

In fact, she had wanted to try to get him home last night, to go round there and make a fuss. But Leonard wouldn't do it.

'Let him stay. After all, he has something to answer. He knew the girl. Wrote her poetry.' That's what he had said.

Sometimes, I feel like killing you, Dr Zeman, she thought. Quite possibly you feel the same about me, and being doctors we both have the means to do it efficiently.

Now she negotiated the turn into Feather Street, drove past the dairy, hit the kerb but then parked the car with some neatness.

'I've made some coffee,' she said, 'and I'll cook you breakfast. I've taken the day off from my clinic.'

The home which Felicity Zeman had created in Feather Street was warm and buoyant and full of light. It rested on the hill like a ship, quite unlike the solid household of Kay Zeman and its heavy antiques and dark curtains.

The family lived on the first floor, leaving the lower rooms for Dr Zeman's consulting rooms.

The small white peke Arthur emerged to greet them with a fury of enthusiastic barks.

'You're home now, love,' Felicity said, putting her arm round her son's shoulders. 'It's over.'

Or that bit was.

Leonard Zeman heard their voices and came up from his consulting room below. 'Glad you're back, Tim. You got him all right then, Fe?' He poured himself some coffee and took a piece of the toast she had made. 'Any press around? Any photographers? He was holding on to his son's arm as if he didn't want to let go.

'Some. But I drove past them fast.'

They had got a picture through the car window, though, of her furious, intent face and Tim staring straight ahead. Tomorrow it would be in some newspaper.

'Any here?'

'No. All clear.'

He hung around, wanting to stay with them to offer love and reassurance but not finding the words, as alas, he so often did with his patients whom he treated and sometimes cured, but could not love. Of course, you weren't obliged to love your patients, only work for them. Better not to love, in fact, but family you were obliged to love. Damn it, he did love them. He took another piece of toast and shared it with Tim.

Felicity became irritated, tried to hold it back and failed. 'Haven't you got any patients?'

'A queue of them.' Some of them ill, others there to view the father of the Zeman boy, so that they could say, 'I was in there yesterday and he looked all right, you wouldn't know there was anything wrong.'

Funny thing, family, he reflected. Tim whom I love, Felicity whom I also love, and Val whom I actually want. Want quite a lot.

'I think I'll have a bath,' said Tim. 'Wash the smell away. Then I suppose I'd better get down to some work. Catch up with things. I've got an exam coming up.'

'Use my bathroom,' said his mother. 'It's looking rather good at the moment. There's a bowl of lily of the valley that just matches the curtains.' Things mattered to her, helped her if necessary. Her spirits could be raised by a nicely arranged breakfast table with the right china.

'Lily of the valley bath oil, too?' asked Tim, trying to get up a smile.

'Of course,' said Felicity, hoping not to show that she thought him pathetic and brave.

The telephone rang, the private line, as Tim went upstairs.

'Wonder who that is?' said Leonard Zeman.

Felicity made no move to answer the bell. 'At a guess, Val.'

The Zeman family were all getting back to normal. Or trying to, well aware that it was not going to be easy, but trying to pretend otherwise.

Soon the news spread around that Tim was back home. When Val heard she told her aunt. Soon Harold and Phil Darbyshire knew, and the Annecks, all of them even the dog, and the dog-walker, Jim Marsh.

They were all trying to hang on to normality in very difficult circumstances. Working, watching television, going to bed. Cooking meals, even eating them. Hanging on. ——

Harder for some than others.

FRED KINVER HAD retired to his home after his interview with John Coffin, where his wife watched him nervously, and waited for results. He was confident. There would be an arrest.

None came. Presently, he realized that it was never going to come. The police were not going to arrest Tim Zeman.

They had no evidence.

Fred Kinver sat crying, watched anxiously by his wife, who cried inside herself only.

In the neighbourhood feelings began to run high. It was known that a man was still in detention. He now had a name: Solomon Wild, and a medical history but no police record. Word about this seeped out. Why was he not being charged? With something, with anything?

The questioning of Tim Zeman and then his release had provoked angry comment in certain quarters. Too middle-class to get charged, was the feeling.

This police inaction speedily produced another outburst from the Paper Man. He was soon to give himself this name.

Two identically phrased letters went off this time, one to John Coffin's office and another to his home in St Luke's Mansions. The Paper Man was making doubly sure his message got through.

# FIVE

*Thursday, June 8*

FRED KINVER would have found it hard to believe that John Coffin could stop thinking about the murder of Anna Mary (Kinver couldn't do so himself), but the truth was that Coffin had learnt to put different bits of his life into different compartments. He hadn't exactly forgotten about the murder, that wasn't how it went, it was part of his job, but he had other and possibly more pressing things to think about.

Nevertheless, when DI Archie Young had met him just as he was getting into his car to drive home, he had a bit of information to pass on. In fact, two pieces.

'Got an ID on the man we're holding, sir. He's Solomon Wild, seems to be his real name too. He's missing from a clinic where he was having treatment.'

'Thought there'd be a background of that sort.'

'Yes, looked likely. We're holding him, though, because there's a charge of arson hanging over him. He set fire to the clinic before he left. And that suits us, because he knows something about the Kinver killing. Either he saw it himself or someone told him about it.'

You take your pick, Coffin thought.

But Archie Young was still talking.

'And we've got something else, sir. I had a bright idea, thought we should have another look round the girl's room. So I started another search of the cupboards and drawers. She had a lot of stuff. Spent money on clothes and shoes. Got a woman detective to go in and look, see what she saw. Woman's eye and all that.'

Coffin waited, car key in hand.

'She came back with the info that several of the girl's shoes were missing. One out of several pairs was gone. Same like the silver slipper. The mother couldn't explain it. Interesting, isn't it?'

Young looked bright-eyed and expectant.

'It was the left silver shoe that went, wasn't it? What about the other shoes? Always the left?'

Young shook his head. 'Right shoe, left shoe. She liked shoes. One gone out of each of four pairs. Makes you think, doesn't it?'

That someone was faking it? To make it look as though the killer knew her well enough to have taken other shoes? Would her father do that to provide evidence against Tim Zeman?

'No one knew that we would be coming in for another search,' said Young, half answering his unspoken query. 'I suddenly decided to do it.'

So supposing it was real? In which case, someone, somewhere had a collection of shoes.

'It makes me think I don't know what to think,' said Coffin. It would be as well to establish when the shoes went. 'Find out,' he said. 'If you can. What about the mother? How did she react? Was she surprised?'

'Surprised,' said Young. 'And frightened.'

COFFIN DROVE BACK to St Luke's Mansions. He also had a life to enjoy. At the moment he was having a

drink in his own sitting-room with Stella Pinero and
Sir Harry. He was enjoying himself.

The Paper Man, who was to prove a shrewd psy-
chologist, no doubt reckoned on all this.

Hence the two letters.

'I love the view from your windows,' said Stella.
'Roofs and tree-tops and just a hint of the river beyond.' She was leaning out of the open window. An
empty glass on the table beside her. 'I mean, you can
smell it.'

'I think that smell's from a canal,' said Coffin,
pouring some wine into her glass.

'You ought to photograph this view, Harry,' she
went on.

'Done a few local street scenes for Dick to use in the
gallery. He's got three blown up to put on the wall as
you go in. You must see them. But faces are more my
thing, you know. I'd like to do one of you, Stella, if
you'd allow.'

'Love it,' said Stella. 'Only let me get my hair done.'
She ran a hand through her hair which she was growing for her part in *Cavalcade*.

'Not your best face, Stella,' said Sir Harry. 'I want
to take you when you are completely off guard. No
make-up, nothing. Looking your worst.'

'Oh, thanks.'

'It will only be what *you* call your worst,' he continued gravely. 'In fact, you will be perfectly beautiful.'

Stella considered the offer. She was not going to
refuse. To be photographed by Harry Beauchamp,
made-up or unmade-up, represented a great prize. But
she did not wish to go down to history looking like the
Witch of Endor.

'I'd like to do you too, sir, if I could,' said Sir Harry, looking at Coffin.

The hand pouring him some more chilled white wine wavered. *Sir, he called me sir. He's older than I am.* Then Coffin decided to take it as a tribute to his rank and authority. Also, Sir Harry was a notable prankster and, come to think of it, was having a good time at both his expense and Stella's. His hand steadied.

'Sounds a good idea. Want me in uniform? I have a rather grand one I wear on special occasions like meeting the Queen.'

'Just head and shoulders, I thought,' said Sir Harry. 'Against a blank wall.'

'Ah yes, a mug shot.'

'Do you know, I think that may have been at the back of my mind,' said Sir Harry with an air of surprise.

'Lay off them, Harry,' said his friend Dick, from near the door where he was talking to Raina Morgan, the youngest, newest and prettiest recruit to Stella's team in the Theatre Workshop. She had trained in the Drama Department of the new University and had been brought in to help direct the production after *Cavalcade*, the play closest (at that moment) to Stella's changeable heart. Although she was constant enough in theatre matters, only with men was she fickle. The play was *The Madras House*. There was a fair turnover in the Theatre Workshop company, people came in for a time, for the fun of it, then moved on. Everyone agreed it was a marvellous experience, but you did need more money.

It suited Stella to run this changing team, it was what she was good at. Stella herself drifted away at times doing a film, a TV series, or a short London run, but all the while leaving a suitable stand-in in charge. She and Coffin's sister Letty had a kind of unspoken arrangement (Letty shrank frugally and sensibly away from long-term contracts) that Stella should direct the Theatre Workshop's operations while, and only while, it suited her. There were advantages on both sides: Letty got a first-class theatrical brain at a bargain price, and Stella got a base, which to an actress of her age and standing was of inestimable value. She had been around long enough to know the worth to her of St Luke's Theatre Workshop. And what was more, she was in pole position to win the race to direct the main theatre when built.

'You can photograph me any way you like, Harry,' said Stella quickly. 'It's a compliment to be asked.' She was already visualizing the big blown-up version she would use in the foyer of the new theatre, when built, and the article in *Vogue* which would precede it.

Footsteps sounded on his stairs and three other people, whom their host vaguely recognized, came into the room. One of them was carrying a bottle and wearing a hopeful smile.

Coffin suddenly felt tired. He detected the signs of a party assembling itself. He had not invited anyone except Stella, who had said could she bring Sir Harry to see the lovely views. With Sir Harry had come Dick, who somehow had Raina with him because she was interested in an artist he was exhibiting, and the rest had just come.

Even after all these years of knowing Stella Pinero he was amazed how easily a party with drinks could set itself up around her. She was at the door now, ushering people in and laughing.

Why not in her own place?

'Don't be sour, dear,' she said, coming up.

'I'm not.'

'Yes, you are. I can see it in your face.' Stella sighed. 'I'm miserable anyway, my poor Mrs Kinver is ill and I'm not surprised. Make them get on with that murder. Clearing it up, I mean.'

'I know what you mean all right.'

Lily Goldstone put her face round the door. 'Hello, is it a party?'

'Lily, welcome. I didn't know you were visiting.' He was pleased to see her, she was one of his favourite people in spite of her well-known and radical views on the police, their behaviour and people's rights. 'In fact, I didn't know you were back.'

Lily had been in New York. 'My play collapsed,' she said in disgust. 'Don't pretend you didn't know. Stella knows. Delighted, weren't you, love, you told me it would.'

'Not delighted,' said Stella. 'But I didn't think it would do. Too English.'

'Loved me, hated the play.' Lily, descendant of a long line of players, one of whom had been a royal mistress, so that Lily claimed royal as well as revolutionary blood, was a great ornament to the European theatre but a very poor judge of a good play. 'I had money in it too, damn it.'

'Come and work for me,' said Stella.

'I was hoping you'd say that, I could do something good for you, not *Cavalcade*, of course, that's not for me, but something really worthy of me. You must pay me a bit better than last time. Or, I tell you what, let's do a deal. Play and film.'

It was what she had come for, Stella concluded.

'Let's talk about it,' she said cautiously.

Lily had something in her hand which she now handed over to her host. 'Found this on the floor downstairs. The door was open.'

There was no name on the envelope, just the command: *Open.*

Inside was a message built up from roughly cut out letters, none of which matched in colour or style. It said: *You are getting it all wrong still. If you won't act then I will.*

This time there was a kind of signature. Not handwritten, but planted across the page in more carefully cut letters, matching in size if not in colour, as if the name mattered to the communicator.

From *The Paper Man*, it said.

Lily and Stella were deep in conversation, still talking plays and films and TV percentages. The word residuals seemed to worry them greatly, so that they were not noticing anything, he thought. He put the letter in his pocket.

Stella swung round at once. 'What is it?'

'Nothing. Just a lunatic letter. I get them sometimes.'

'Don't we all,' said Lily, who actually had sent one or two in her time. For political purposes, naturally.

'Come on,' said Stella, 'don't let it spoil the party.'

But the Paper Man had already done that.

Coffin looked out of his open window. He could just see the gardens of Feather Street, and he could hear a dog barking. Then another joined in. He thought he could hear a distant bell ringing.

By now he was enough of a local to know that meant that Jim Marsh was about to take one of the battling Jack Russells out for a walk.

# SIX

*Friday, June 9, through to Saturday evening*

JIM MARSH HAD given himself a few days off from the Poly, where he was, anyway, an unpredictable student, not given to taking his work too seriously. He was clever, good at chemistry, physics, and biology as well as being a proficient mathematician, these being the subjects he was required to study if he hoped to get into veterinary school.

He'd manage it, he could cope with the theory, no sweat. But he was more interested in people and animals, his mother's son after all. She had been passionately interested in people in the mass, especially if abandoned in India or starving in Africa, but somewhat more negligent of those close at hand. Jim hadn't really minded, he'd understood her dreams. Even her nightmares, and certainly her suicide. If she'd killed his father, as seemed likely at one time, he'd have understood that too.

He couldn't forgive old Kinver for the names he had called his mother. One name in particular. Whatever his mother was, she hadn't been that. Never another man in her life except his father as far as Jim knew, well, possibly one or two, but nothing to count, she just had mad ideas and shouted them out. Scared people like old Kinver who felt frightened, anyway. He was a pig. Mrs Kinver was all right, but Anna Mary had deserved a better father than that one.

Come to think of it, he deserved a better father himself. But there were some problems you could do something about and others you could not. His father, now asleep after the early milk round which exhausted him for the rest of the day, was one such.

Jim put a casserole in the oven for the evening meal, he was a good cook, he'd had to learn and found the skill had come easily to him. He had collected recipes from the Feather Street ladies and got on with it. Mrs Anneck had taught him how to make a meat loaf, Felicity Zeman how to make gazpacho and Val Humberstone particularly nice and rich chocolate cakes. That was his repertoire. Now he took a bowl of stewed mince with him for Jumbo's supper. He was convinced that Jumbo's terrible aggression was due to what he was given to eat.

'You are what you eat,' said Jim. 'You live by it and you die by it. That is a self-evident truth.'

In that case, he wondered what John Coffin, whom he had been observing closely, ate that his father did not and whether he should try to do the same himself. In an unfriendly way, he admired the Chief Commander. 'We ought to assassinate him,' his mother had cried, without any intention of planting any bombs. Jim did not agree here, he saw the man as doing a good job. You might not admire the job itself, but to see it well done was something.

'It's no good, though,' he told himself. 'I'm not that side of the law and never will be. It's in the blood.' His mother, possibly because she had been the child of a successful lawyer, had been a passionate protester against the police. She and Lily Goldstone had met on many a barricade. But Lily had a life force running strongly through her and Clare Marsh had not.

Jim woke his father before going out to walk the Feather Road dogs. 'Dad, turn the oven down in half an hour, will you?'

His father opened his eyes. 'Where are you off to? Where are you all hours of the day? I never see you.'

Jim shrugged. 'I think I'm around most of the time.'

'Then you ought to be at school.' You could never win with his father. 'What's that you've got under your arm?'

'Just something I've cooked.' He made for the door before his father could look. 'Don't forget the casserole. I've got to go round to Mr Dibbin's after I've walked the dogs.' John Dibbin was the local vet for whom he did odd jobs. 'He wants me to deliver some medicines.'

'Heard you banging around in the kitchen. What were you up to?'

'Just tidying up, Dad.' And Jim escaped into the garden and out what he called the 'Dog Run', the path between the houses owned by the Annecks, the Darbyshires and the Zemans, linking one back garden to the next.

'You've got a hidey-hole somewhere,' muttered his father before sinking back into sleep. He'd been up since dawn, he needed his sleep. His initial idea that he would rise early for his milk round, then have the rest of the day to spend writing his novel, or his play, or the poem sequence, had not worked out. He was always too tired. I ought to have been a brain surgeon, he thought.

JIM WAS METHODICAL in the walking of the dogs. He took them in the same order every day, beginning with

Felicity Zeman's white peke, which hated to go out and usually had to be carried outward so he could hurry back home. Then came Val's mongrel Bob, followed by Edie and then Jumbo. He always took Jumbo last because he was so aggressive, also because Jim disliked Jumbo as much as Jumbo appeared to dislike him. Not that one could tell for sure with Jumbo, who seemed willing to take on the world.

All the dogs went on the same walk which they knew thoroughly by heart and somewhat resented, especially Jumbo who was the most intelligent of the dogs as well as the crossest.

The food for Jumbo was by way of an experiment to see if it sweetened his temper. So far it did not appear to have worked.

Handing out food, a tidbit here, a trifle there, for he could not ignore the other animals, Jim got on with the job with his usual briskness. He did not linger anywhere much except in the Zemans' kitchen. If he liked one of the animals at all, it was Bob, the mongrel.

When Val Humberstone came into the kitchen, he said to her: 'I wonder if I could have my money today. What I've earned.' It was two days off payday, which was usually the end of the week.

'Sure.' Val fetched her purse.

'There's something I want to buy.'

'You don't have to explain to me. Glad to do it. I might be away at the weekend anyway.'

Jim received his money politely, but did not smile. He was, as Val had observed before, an unsmiling, grave-faced boy. And she for one did not blame him.

She liked boys, she was fond of her nephew Tim, although he did get himself into troubles. This was not, at the moment, a very good time for the Zemans.

She stood in the kitchen and picked up the telephone. She dialled Stella Pinero's number. Not there.

Val looked at the big old clock on the wall. She might be at the theatre. No matinée today and too early for the evening performance to have started, but Stella was probably there. Was Stella still in the show in London or had she come back to the Workshop? Val couldn't be sure. She tried the theatre.

The bright voice of the young stage manager answered her. 'No, Stella's not here yet. She was going somewhere with Sir Harry Beauchamp. He's doing some photographs of the site of the new theatre.'

Wonder where she is, thought Val. Like to talk to her. She might tell me what to say, or even what not to say, to her policeman friend John Coffin.

There was something she wanted to pass on to the police, needed to pass on. Just speculation really, the police might believe her or might not (that cocky young Detective-Inspector Young certainly would not), but John Coffin might.

She had met him once with Stella and thought him a believing kind of person.

She went back into the sitting-room where her Aunt Kay was sitting on the sofa. She hadn't been too well these last few days. She was having treatment for her heart condition which was supposed to be responding well.

'Auntie, do you think you ought to have eaten so many of those cakes?' Several small chocolate cakes had gone.

'They were so good,' said Kay Zeman. 'Better than usual. Your cooking is coming on.' She sounded sleepy.

'Thanks.' Val picked up the tea-tray and carried it into the kitchen. She often made these little biscuity chocolate cakes. They were put together out of crisp crushed biscuit stirred into melted chocolate. A few nuts made them crunchy.

'I think I'll go to bed early.'

Val turned her head alertly. 'Do you want the doctor?'

Leonard's partner, Roger Eaton, treated Kay Zeman, while Val took herself off to another outfit altogether. Leonard did not look after his own family: not good professional practice.

'No,' said old Mrs Zeman stoutly. 'Just early bed.'

'I'll help you up.'

'Don't bother.' Kay Zeman struggled up the stairs, took out her teeth and quietly put herself to bed. She was beginning to feel very sleepy and heavy, but as a doctor's widow she made light of her own ailments. You were trained to by years of no one wanting to know that you were ill.

In the night, her heart became arrhythmic, she was already unconscious, soon she ceased to breathe and quietly died.

LEONARD ZEMAN, summoned by Val, stood by his mother's bed and looked down at her. There were no tears in his eyes, but Val had been crying. She looked shaken and white.

He stretched out a hand and gripped hers. 'Don't worry, you did your best. She loved you too, that counts. Her heart was bad, you know. She could have gone any time.'

'But you didn't think so.' It was a statement, not a question.

'You can never tell. I'll have to call Roger. She was taking the tablets he sent round?' Val nodded. 'He'll do the death certificate. No need for an inquest, thank goodness.'

'Oh, no,' said Val who hadn't even considered it.

Natural death is always easier on the family. Fred Kinver could have told them both that.

FRED KINVER heard the news at breakfast as he read his daily paper. His wife had heard from the milkman who thought she ought to know. She was not usually on talking terms with Chris Marsh—who was?—but he meant this kindly, as she recognized.

She told Fred and with a sinking heart saw the gleam flash across his face. A locking-in day again, she told herself. Well, my lad, I've had another key made and you won't shut me in so easily.

'Gone, has she?' said Fred, going back to his cup of tea. 'That's one of them away, then.' He sounded pleased.

'Heart, the milkman said.'

'It would be, wouldn't it?'

'In her sleep last night. His son told him.'

'I wonder how he knew?'

'Went round with something for one of the dogs, I expect. And Miss Val would tell him.'

'Miss Val, Miss Val,' mocked her husband angrily. 'Don't talk like a servant. You ought to hate them all, all those Zemans.'

'I can't, Fred. I know you can, but I can't.'

He stirred his tea. 'The police were worse than use-less with those Zemans. Someone else had to take a hand.'

'Who, Fred?'

The tea swirled round the cup one way and then another. 'God, I suppose,' said Fred Kinver. He but-tered a piece of toast, more to do something than to eat it.

'I like it when God shows his hand,' he said.


JOHN COFFIN HEARD the news from Mimsie Marker as he bought his morning newspaper from her.

'That's interesting.' He stared at the newspaper headline which was about riots in China.

'Why?' asked Mimsie. 'By the way, the Tube's on strike. If you wanted to use it, you'll have to walk.'

'It's always interesting when someone in the circle of people connected with a violent death dies.'

'Coincidence, you mean?'

'Yes, if you like.' Whatever coincidence meant in that context. It meant movement, and in a murder case anything was better than stalemate.

'It was her heart,' said Mimsie. 'So I've heard.'

He took his newspaper round to Max's Delicates-sen and asked for coffee and hot toast.

Max too had heard of the death. He was a small, neat man, reputed to be a Czech but now the com-plete Thameswater Londoner. He had a tall, plump Italian wife, who was hardly ever seen but who was known to be at work in the background, and three daughters, growing up fast, over whom he attempted, unsuccessfully as a rule, to operate a fatherly disci-pline. He knew that they did a lot of things he would disapprove of, behaved in ways that would have shocked his mother (long dead, God rest her soul), and could only hope now that they would never find it necessary to tell him what they got up to.

'I shall miss Mrs Zeman,' he said, planting a small coffee-pot and a jug of cream on the marble tabletop. 'Nice lady. Good customer too. She knew what a cheesecake should be.'

'Good cook, was she?' said Coffin, pouring out some coffee while he waited for the toast. Presently a hand pushed a plate round the door. Mrs Max, presumably; the hand wore a wedding ring.

'Couldn't cook a thing. Val did most of it.'

Across the room Coffin could see Stella Pinero, wearing dark spectacles and pretending not to see him. This happened sometimes, usually in the morning, and meant she had no make-up on, and not looking her best, and he was not to know her.

'Who told you?' asked Coffin.

Max nodded towards Stella in the corner. 'Miss Pinero. Val Humberstone telephoned her with the news.'

Coffin drank his coffee and ate his toast, taking care not to notice Stella when suddenly the rules were changed and she was there at his table.

'Hello, good morning.' She sounded distracted. 'Don't worry about me, just casting problems with *Cavalcade*. Lily Goldstone is being very legalistic about the new play.' Lily would be, she always was, as many a police picket-line could attest. 'Money too. I can tell you that your sister Letty is a hard bargainer.'

'I know that better than you do.' The flat in which he lived in St Luke's Mansions was a part of the development of the old church initiated by his half sister Lætitia, but blood had given no bargains and he had paid a full price.

'Who'd be an actress and a director all rolled into one?'

Or policeman either, Chief Commander of a new Force? He had his problems: today a committee of Members of Parliament would be visiting him. He would give them lunch, then take them around. It was supposed to be a friendly inspection, but he had no doubt sharp questions would follow. You couldn't keep politics out of his life.

Then there was the problem with a difficult subordinate, a man hard to work with but with valuable technical skills that were needed. He must try to hang on to Chief Inspector A. Swapping, while not letting him make the lives of those he worked with unendurable.

As Coffin himself was one of these, it was quite a problem, but one he was prepared to tackle with vigour.

But underneath all this, he was concerned at the emotional divisions in the population he was policing, the growing divide between the old docklanders and the newcomers, who were felt to be too rich and too pushy. This stress was finding a focus in the Kinver case.

There was a growing feeling about the lack of progress in getting the killer of Anna Mary Kinver. Or specifically, a positive feeling that they were going easy on Timmy Zeman.

The Zemans, like the Kinvers, were an old-established family, but they were well off, and that seemed to put them on the other side of the ravine.

Stella took a deep breath, reminding him that she was a forlorn and worried actress. 'It's too much for one woman. I have too much responsibility.'

'It's the breath of life to you,' Coffin said to Stella.

Probably the same could be said of Coffin himself. He liked what he did, enjoyed it more every day, and thought he got better at it. But he missed the cases he had worked on, he had enjoyed prowling round an investigation, asking questions, watching people. He was aware that he still did behave like this and that some of his officers thought he should keep his nose out of a case, any case.

He had no doubt that both Paul Lane and Archie Young felt that way now, but Paul was an old friend with whom he had worked many times. They had a history together.

Archie Young was different: full of ambition, he probably resented being asked to discuss the Kinver case, but he would be too canny to show it.

'But that's not what I wanted to talk to you about,' Stella was saying. 'You've heard that Kay Zeman's dead?' He nodded in reply. 'I've had Val on the telephone, she has something to tell you. I don't think she wants to do it, but she seems to feel she must.'

'About her aunt?'

'No, I don't think so.' Stella paused. 'From what she said, it's about the murder of Anna Mary Kinver.'

WHEN COFFIN ARRIVED in his office and before looking at the letters and messages which were already waiting for him, he telephoned Superintendent Paul Lane.

'How are things going in the Kinver case?'

There was a pause. 'Young keeps you in touch? He's meant to.'

'Yes, he drops bits of information at intervals. But what's really going on?' If anything.

'A bit of a doldrums.'

'I'm anxious about the pressures building up. There's a lot of feeling building up. Them and Us. An idea we're not really pursuing the Zeman lad too hard.'

'Not true.'

'I know that. But politically, I need a result. Or anyway, something. What's your feeling about the Zeman's boy, is he guilty?'

'We can prove anything.'

'But you think Yes?'

'There's a difference of opinion. I think Yes, Young thinks No.'

'Valerie Humberstone wants to see me. She claims she has something to tell me.'

'Ah. I reckon we might know what that's about.'

'Well, what?'

'She used to go to the disco where Anna Mary and the boy Tim and the Anneck kids and the Darbyshire boys went. She helped there. The disco is an offshoot of a youth club she was interested in. We've picked up the idea that she saw someone with Anna Mary once or twice. She might be going to tell us about that. Harold Darbyshire goes down there to help occasionally.'

'Is that a loaded statement?'

Lane laughed. 'I wouldn't say that. All the Feather Street crowd took an interest in the disco at one time, although I believe they've given it up now and gone on to other things, like the theatre, but Harold was down there most often, apart from Val Humberstone.' In a detached voice, he added: 'Helped the girl with her computer studies, I gather.'

LATER THAT EVENING he took one of his walks, quietly inspecting by moonlight the province in which he was responsible for keeping the Queen's Peace. This habit had earned him the code name of WALKER: he knew his progress was observed and mapped, so that a sigh of relief went up when the silent watchers could report: WALKER is back home. But so far he had never been mugged or even threatened. Sometimes he had seen dark shadows melt away down side roads, but he had never been approached.

His territory stretched on both sides of the River Thames, touching Wapping and Poplar on one boundary and reaching Rotherhithe and Bermondsey on the other. All old Anglo-Saxon villages in origin where once manors and monastic estates had stretched towards the river, now heavily populated urban villages like those in the New City. Westwards was the ancient City of London itself where his writ did not run.

But this area of Leathergate, Spinnergate, Swinehythe and Easthythe was large enough for him.

Within his fiefdom were St Saviour's Dock, which was probably pre-Roman and in its day in the thirteenth century had been the busiest dock in London; at the other end of his area, Coffin was responsible for the peace in the Great Eastern Dock, whose splendid Victorian structures were now carefully preserved buildings, housing offices and luxury apartments. Coffin could not have afforded to live there himself, but his rich sister Letty had just taken one for herself and her daughter.

In addition, he had several hospitals, one exceedingly famous for specialist attention to neonates, and one which was setting itself to deal with diseases like typhoid and malaria and cholera, afflictions hardly seen in the other London, but coming back to his New City with its varied and wandering population. He had a fledgling university. Hundreds of schools. Churches, chapels, mosques, temples and house churches, whatever you could have in the religious line, he had. There were several museums, more than one art gallery, a theatre, and numberless bingo halls, disco clubs and straightforward drinking clubs.

Servicing all these activities were ambulances, street cleaners and firemen, all looking to him to keep the streets peaceful so they could go about their work.

He had a rich population, he had a poor population, and they rubbed shoulders with some irritation on both sides. There were numerous ethnic groups, a flourishing criminal community with its roots going back through the centuries, and a floating population of drunks and itinerants of both sexes.

Sometimes they all shook down together peacefully enough. At other times, as now, there was friction.

At the back of his mind was another and darker worry. It was the gulf between his Force and the population from which, with increasing strength, they felt separated. The police had their world, but it was apart and outside the civil world in which they lived, married, had their houses with mortgages like anyone else, and sent their children to school. Professionally, they lived in a rough, tough, brutal world in which they were required to show all the virtues of compassion and sympathy while getting precious little back from the community they served.

It had always been the same, but it was hard and getting harder. This was one of John Coffin's major anxieties.

Considering all this, he found he was walking past the patch of allotments south of Elder Street, by the Brazen Head Docks and near the railway yard. He could smell earth and damp vegetables. Each patch was the treasured possession of some keen gardener, threatened now, because any day a developer might sweep in to create several more row of houses. On every allotment was a hut or lean-to such as the one used as his 'office' by Fred Kinver. He probably was not alone in this, they were well-known refuges and hiding places. On most nights you could be sure of finding the odd dosser. One old woman seemed to live there permanently, and however often she was 'rescued' by the social services or the Salvation Army, always found her way back.

In the distance he heard a cat yowling and another feline voice answering it. Animal life abounded around here. He had met a fox once, face to face in a side-street.

Without conscious thought his feet had taken him towards Rope Alley, quiet and empty now in the moonlight. A dull, dark, little passage between two bright thoroughfares where the traffic never stopped rolling.

Then he was approaching the old Lead Works, now an art gallery. It was a fine building, but so far he had not been inside it. An invitation to a Private View of Dockland Art rested on his desk, as yet unanswered. He remembered that Sir Harry had been photographing street scenes about the time of the murder. It might be worth a look at those pictures.

At first he had thought of the death of Anna Mary Kinver as one of those cases with firm boundaries like a box. It might or might not be solved but there would be an end to it. A self-limiting disease.

Now he had the unnerving feeling that this was just a beginning, and that the affair was growing all round him.

In one of those little huts on the allotments, just passed by John Coffin, the Paper Man was at work. He was laboriously putting together an archive. He typed slowly with one hand.

DEATH NUMBER ONE, he typed.

Then he added the date, and the quantity of poison used. Not where he had obtained the poison, that would be telling.

Then he rolled up what he had written in a plastic sheet and, like a dog, he buried it.

Like a dog, he knew exactly where he had buried it. Would dig it up when needed, and had left minute signs, but careful ones, where it could be found.

You might find it yourself.

# SEVEN

*Friday, June 16, through to Saturday*

THE DEATH OF Mrs Zeman cast a cloud over the community of Feather Street. In her time she had quarrelled with most of them, but always made it up again. She was a respected and even admired figure. It was a tense time even though Feather Street did not, of course, know of the sinister letter to John Coffin from the Paper Man.

Now they felt they had two sadnesses to mourn: first the murder of Anna Mary Kinver and now the death of Kay Zeman.

Instructed in tact by his superiors, Detective-Inspector Archie Young had decided to leave the Zemans alone until after the funeral, but a discreet eye was kept on the household. Dr Zeman handed his work over to his assistant for the time being, Timmy Zeman kept to the house, and only Felicity went off to her clinics as usual, she said you couldn't ignore sick children no matter what. And, naturally, Arthur the white peke went out for his walks also as usual. He could not be ignored either.

Councillor Mary Anneck was absent from several of her committees and her son Peter and her daughter and the daughter's boyfriend held back from playing loud pop music. Only the dog Edie carried on with life as normal, taking her walks and snarling at Jumbo.

Jumbo spent a lot of time in his kennel where Philippa had tethered him as a mark of mourning.

The dog Bob, on the other hand, got even more walks, petting and extra tidbits because everyone was sorry for him. So much Kay's dog, they said, he loved her, he must be missing her. He was living the life of Riley.

The Marshes, father and son, carried on much as before, but Chris Marsh had concluded that the Zemans would not be drinking as much milk as before and, unasked, cut down his delivery to both households to one pint a day. Jim walked the dogs as always, since dogs have their own ways of getting their revenge if walks are denied them. Feather Street valued its carpets and furnishings too much to make life awkward for their demanding pets. Anyway, Jim, who respected the animals, would have done the job.

Feather Street had a thoroughly uneasy feeling about the death of Kay. Shouldn't have come just now, they thought. She wouldn't have wanted it. She would have wanted to stay around and protect her beloved grandson Timmy.

On the other hand, the communal but largely unexpressed view was that it was lucky for Val. Oh, she was miserable, in spite of their quarrels she had loved the old lady. They were pretty sure she had loved her, that is, but she had certainly been a barrier to her affair with Leonard Zeman.

They knew all about that business even if they did not talk about it much. On the whole they thought it would be nice for Leonard to have Val as his wife in place of that Felicity who was never home looking after son, dog or husband, but always absent doing good elsewhere, one presumed. Feather Street was public-spirited but thought home should come first.

Over coffee in her kitchen Councillor Mary Anneck said as much to Phil Darbyshire. They were back from the funeral.

'Val'll get some good out of it. Leonard will divorce Felicity.'

'Do you think so?' She crumbled one of Mary Anneck's famous dry shortbread biscuits. Biscuits in the Anneck household were either dry and stale or soft and stale. She was noted for it. Philippa had made the coffee herself, so it was hot and strong.

'They'll come to some arrangement.' With annoyance Phil saw Mary Anneck pour water into the coffee to weaken it and then milk to cool it. Good food was wasted on Mary, she actually preferred the poor stuff. 'Kay was the real stumbling block for Leonard. For Val too, probably. Emotionally, I mean. Marvellous the control that old lady had over them all.'

'I liked her, though, didn't you? I was terrified of her when we first came to live here, but after a while I saw all the warmth and mirth under the sharpness.'

'Oh, she was a warrior all right. They don't build them like that any more.' Long years on public committees had taught Mary the art of the cliché. She spoke in well-used clumps of words, knowing she did it. It was a kind of shorthand and it saved her the trouble of thinking when she was miserable or disturbed as she was now. She didn't want to think there was any connection between the death of Kay Zeman and the death of Anna Mary Kinver, but she couldn't help wondering underneath.

Phil said it openly: 'You don't think she thought Tim had killed the girl and that brought on the heart attack?'

'She never believed he did it.' Mary's tone was tentative. In her opinion, Kay Zeman could easily believe her grandson guilty of rape and murder. In her long life she had seen many terrible things happen to nice people, and known of nice people doing horrible things. Her generation, her race, had had to face that reality. Kay anyway had proclaimed her readiness to believe in the evil of the human animal.

'She might have known something.'

'Ah,' Mary took one of her own biscuits and, finding it hard and dry, absently dunked it in her coffee, now nicely chilled, to soften it. 'Come on, you've got something on your mind. Tell Mary.'

'Val knows something. She told Stella Pinero she wanted to talk to the police but didn't know how to set about it.'

'You just go down and start talking.'

'She wanted to be sure of talking to the right person, of course. She knew Stella knows John Coffin.'

He was a familiar figure in the neighbourhood. He lived in St Luke's Mansions, he was often at the Theatre Workshop, he was a friend of Stella Pinero (some said more than that), and Mimsie Marker had pronounced him a good bloke. Not one of your common policemen.

'Ah. Val say anything to you?'

Phil shook her head. 'No, that's what makes me think it's serious information. Hard evidence.'

About Timmy Zeman? Mary Anneck chewed over the thought. Would Val tell anything she knew about her nephew? Tentatively, she put her own position.

'I've had a word with Peter and Hester, they seem in the clear. Hadn't seen much of Anna Mary for quite a while. These teenage relationships do come and go, you know. Hester says Andrew, that's her current boy, never knew Anna at all. Well, by sight, but not to speak to. They do seem a bit tentative about Timmy, though. Something there but I can't quite get at it.'

If Phil thought Mary was too trusting about her own brood (and she did), she didn't say so. 'You've got to believe in your own children,' she said slowly. 'That's absolutely vital. Terrible repercussions on family life if you don't.' But she knew that she could never be quite sure you saw through to the heart of anyone, not even your own children.

Especially not your own children.

'Harold knew her too, didn't he?' Mary carefully avoided her friend's eyes as she put the question. A sensitive one.

'Taught her a bit. Clever kid. He liked her.' Phil made her voice sound generous, warm.

That was the right way to handle Mary and her query. Sound matter-of-fact, which she didn't actually feel, by the way. A terrible chasm opened beneath her feet every time she considered Anna Mary and Harold.

Phil put the pot of coffee back on the stove and turned on the gas. She had known Mary long enough to take the liberty. In any case, Mary herself was detached about her kitchen. The Annecks' kitchen was full of sun and warmth, lined with excellent equipment largely unused, since Mary opened a tin or a frozen packet whenever she could. A tin-opener was her preferred tool. Philippa herself cooked vegetarian style and that was cooking, as she often said with pride. Not many quick cuts with nuts and legumes.

'So what has Val said?' asked Mary. 'Any idea?'

'She hasn't said anything yet. Kay dying like that . . . didn't seem the time, I suppose.'

Phil had kept a pretty close tab on developments, thought Mary. She was closer to Stella than was Mary herself, who was always so busy with her public duties but yielding to no one in her admiration of Stella as an artist.

'How did you think Val looked?'

'Pretty awful. Didn't look too well at all. I think she's got a bad cold.' It was amazing how often grief and misery translated itself into physical terms. 'Leonard didn't look up to much either. You can never tell with Felicity, she's got those steady good looks.'

'I'd call her hard,' said Mary. From a spot at her foot, Edie gave a low growl. 'Kind but hard.' She dropped a biscuit down to Edie who picked it up to carry to her basket. Presently, defeated by it, she buried it under her blanket. Time would soften it. 'Lovely funeral, wasn't it? Beautiful flowers.'

'Kay would have wanted that.'

'Did you see Fred Kinver at the funeral? Came to the grave. Not Mrs Kinver, just Fred. I didn't like that much.'

Phil put down her mug of coffee, you never got a cup at Mary's, always great thick mugs, and lucky if they weren't chipped. She had even been known to offer disposable plastic beakers. 'Yes, I saw. I didn't care for it either.'

There was a moment while they both sat silent.

Mary said: 'Wonder what Val's got on her mind?'

Phil shook her head. 'No idea. I'd be glad to know. Be glad when we do know.' If ever. 'I identify with Val. Don't you?'

'Don't think so, no, I'm sure I don't. Got too many other worries of my own without taking hers on.'

'Worrying, though, all of it, isn't it?'

'Let's keep our worries to ourselves, shall we, Phil?'

Phil nodded. 'Sure... I've only said something to you because, well, we're all in it together.'

THE FEATHER STREETERS may have thought their worries were private to them, but it was not so.

Versions of their anxieties filtered back to John Coffin, transmitted by Stella Pinero. He had to assume Archie Young knew of them, too.

The fact was that these anxieties were diffused, personalized reflections of lines of inquiry really being pursued by the police.

They were interested in all the young friends of Anna Mary Kinver. This included the Anneck boys, the Darbyshire kids, as well as Tim Zeman, not to mention others from the disco.

They knew of the work that Harold Darbyshire had done with Anna Mary, and they knew that Anna Mary had said, possibly in joke, possibly not, that he was nice but a bit of a creep.

Soloman Wild was on remand; he would be charged with arson for burning down one floor of the Darling Road Hostel for Men. Not forgotten by any means by the police team, who had the feeling that there was gold there if they could only strike it, he had been questioned several times about the murder of Anna Mary. He had ceased to say that he did it, but had added one crucial detail to what had gone on: Anna

Mary had not screamed, nor tried to run away, she had walked slowly towards her killer. So he claimed.

'She knew him, she was walking towards someone she knew and had no need to fear,' Archie Young had said. 'I hate to give Kinver best, he's been a real pain, poor chap, but he may have been right in thinking she named Zeman.'

This had been said at a meeting on the Paper Man (a report of which would go later to John Coffin), chaired by Superintendent Paul Lane and attended by Archie Young together with several colleagues, one a woman sergeant who specialized in crimes against women.

This figure was so far a secret from the general public, although the Press had, somehow, got wind of his existence.

'Larry Hemms of *Newsworld* rang me to ask about it,' reported Young.

'How the devil did he get to know?' said Lane angrily. He liked his security to be tight, and in spite of past experiences really believed it could be managed.

Young shrugged. 'It's his job.'

'Well, I won't ask how he got the information.'

No, don't, thought Archie Young, or I might be obliged to tell you. He suspected a young detective-constable who drank in the same pub as Larry Hemms. He had already warned the chap.

'They haven't printed anything. But that won't last.'

'I'm surprised no newspaper has had a letter,' said someone.

'He might get round to it.'

'Are we assuming that there are going to be other letters?' said Lane tartly.

'I am,' said Young. He was closer to the coal face, as it were, and could feel vibrations coming at him. 'We've had more than one, there'll be others. He's that sort.'

Everyone present had photocopies of the two letters. So far there had been no detailed scientific examination of them, apart from a careful fingerprint check. The always busy police scientists had plenty of other work on hand and, not having been asked to give the letters priority, had not done so, but other tests might come later. It depended on what the Paper Man got up to in the future and how important he was judged to be. At the moment there were suggestions about the magazines and newspapers from which the letters had been cut. A couple of tabloids with colour printing, and the *Radio* and *TV Times* seemed to have been favoured. Everyone had access to them, nothing unusual to seize on there. The letters had been stuck on to poor quality paper, apparently torn from an old notebook. The same notebook in each case.

The notebook was an old one with yellowing pages. It had been around somewhere for a good few years and got stained with some unidentifiable substance. Not badly stained, just spattered here and there. It had a faintly medicinal smell to it.

'Are we taking these letters seriously or not?' asked Lane.

'I am,' said Young. 'I don't know quite what they mean or why they are coming, but I smell trouble.'

He was in there somewhere, doing something, the writer of these letters, and time would show what it was. Young did not know if he hoped this or feared it.

'So what does this "one death" mean? Does he mean the death of Anna Mary Kinver? Or some other death? One we don't know about yet?'

'You tell me,' said Young. 'And one death . . . that implies death two, doesn't it?'

The discussion moved back to the murder of Anna Mary. It was at this point that Archie Young made the remark about Anna Mary and Solomon Wild.

As the meeting drew to an end, and the discussion became desultory, Paul Lane quietly turned off the tape-recorder on his desk.

JOHN COFFIN, who had played the tape-recording of the meeting as soon as he got it that day, had the two letters from the Paper Man on his desk where he could watch them, almost as if he expected them to burst into active and baleful life. He put a paperweight on them absently while he read the minutes of a meeting on Inner City Crime, which he had chaired, and checked the agenda for yet another on finance. He had an excellent financial adviser but he had learnt from experience that the placing of items on the agenda of a meeting was vital. Near the end, when energy was spent was where to place an item on which opposition could be expected. He had a very aggressive local administration and opposition to the police could be counted on. There were one or two items about police expenditure he was anxious to get through and he did not want any sardonic comments about the cost of riot shields.

It all came back to the division in the community he served that worried him so much. Graffiti on the walls, violence on the streets, a feeling of hate. He loved his London, he didn't want it to be like this.

Lately, the property owned by his sister where he lived himself in St Luke's Mansions, as well as the Theatre Workshop and the site for the new theatre, now being dug over, had been the focus for attacks. His own car had been damaged, and the walls of the Theatre Workshop daubed:

*Yuppies go home*, the message had read, *and leave our district to us.*

Stella Pinero had caused it to be wiped out, but next day another message took its place.

*Give us back our territory*, this message had said.

It was gone now, Stella had acted quickly, although she was getting uneasy.

Territory was the heart of it, Coffin thought. Man is a territorial animal. Perhaps even rape was a means of marking his patch.

He put his hand over the letter from the Paper Man. He, and the murderer of Anna Mary Kinver, and people like Solomon Wild, thrown back to community care when the community did not want him and had nowhere to put him, were part of the same problem.

Coffin played the tape of the meeting again, moving it forward to the bit he wanted, and listened to Archie Young's voice recounting Solomon Wild's words.

He reflected on Solomon Wild who had reported that Anna Mary had 'walked towards' her killer.

He would say that, Coffin thought, if she was walking towards him, and he was the attacker. That is what he would see.

Only the forensic evidence protected him. Another man had been the rapist.

Solomon might have been helping, though. Held the girl down while the rape went on.

It was something to be considered. Ideas sprouted in his mind like weeds after rain, none of them pleasant. He did not live in a pleasant world.

He turned the tape back to the discussion on the letter from the Paper Man. He too had wondered what the phrase *Death Number One* meant.

He looked at his watch, time had gone fast, the afternoon was drawing to a close, already his secretary had brought in two trays of tea and taken each away untouched. Val Humberstone was due to call on him in St Luke's Mansions for a drink and a talk later that day.

Was Stella Pinero going to be there? She had set the interview up and would bring Val in, but would probably then tactfully take herself off. That was what he hoped, but you could never be quite sure with Stella, she might feel it her task to stay there and protect Val Humberstone from the wicked police. She said she had no idea what Val wanted to say.

He assumed that it would be something about the death of Anna Mary and the involvement of Timmy Zeman, but it might not be. Val had sat on this communication of hers for some time now, the death of Kay Zeman intervening, but now she wanted to talk.

He took the tape with him, put the letters from the Paper Man (now neatly enclosed in a plastic envelope) in his case, and set out.

He walked home. He was WALKER after all and on foot was a good way to keep an eye on his territory.

There it was, that word again. A good word, a useful word in the right context but dangerous in its content.

He deliberately walked home through Elder Street so that he could see how the Kinver house looked. You could tell sometimes what was going on with the inhabitants from the look of a house.

No. 13 seemed quiet and tidy, the garden needed a thorough weed, but, no gardener himself, this did not worry him. The curtains were drawn back, that was a good sign, the windows all closed, the front door closed. He couldn't see the back door from the road, but he would take a bet that was closed too. Slight touch of fortress mentality there, but to be expected.

He walked on, realizing that he was both hungry and thirsty. And deeply uneasy.

What about the Kinvers? What about the Zemans? What about Feather Street?

FEATHER STREET was miserable. In Elder Street, unaware that John Coffin had just passed through, things were looking up.

Fred Kinver and his wife were in the kitchen which overlooked the rear garden, thus they had not observed the Chief Commander's inspection. Here they were eating a cooked high tea of fish and chips, prepared by Mrs Kinver. Fred was eating with appetite at last.

'I enjoyed the funeral,' he said, buttering a slice of bread and butter.

'Oh, Fred, you shouldn't talk like that.'

'Why not? I did enjoy it. Why shouldn't I? One of them is gone.'

'An old lady, Fred.'

'They were able to bury the old lady, weren't they? We haven't buried Anna Mary yet.'

The police had not yet released for burial their daughter's body, Mrs Kinver closed her eyes, it did not do to dwell on this fact, nor the reasons for it.

'Miss Humberstone didn't look too well,' observed Fred, not without pleasure. 'Pass the jam, will you?'

'Strawberry jam, the make you like, Tiptree. I bought it specially.' She pushed the jar across. 'There's a programme on the Telly tonight you usually watch.' Not quite true, he had not watched it for days now, but it was worth a try. Normality might never come back, but she knew you must make a play for it. 'Or there's that video you enjoy. I like it myself, let's watch it again.' She didn't really like it that much, it was macabre.

Fred's eyes flicked towards the rack where he kept the videos, those he owned and those he borrowed. 'Think I'll pop down the allotment.' He had a packet of cuttings about John Coffin in his pocket which needed sticking in his album. The library had seen a lot of him lately.

'Oh.' She was disappointed. Back to that, she thought; still, he had eaten well and, granted the great misery that still rested on them both, he seemed in better spirits. Not exactly happy, but more positive.

She submitted to being locked in the house if that was a comfort to him, but she had long since provided herself with a key.

If she had to go out, then she would. She always had the fear that some day she would have to rescue Fred from something and that she'd better be ready. He wasn't the strong one in the family, she was.

THE PAPER MAN was also happy. Things were working the way he wanted, justice was being done all round. He was very well aware that his life was, in its own way, running parallel with that of Fred Kinver.

He too was cutting up pieces of newspaper, pasting what he had cut out on other paper. Making messages.

He too had a spot he called his own in the allotments. Not far from Fred Kinver, very close to Fred Kinver's.

That same evening, he too was there. Inside Fred's office, as a matter of fact, although a little later than Fred, and pretty pleased with himself.

Almost all would be revealed in due course. He felt himself to be in charge of the scene. He was pulling the strings and the puppets were moving according to his desires.

When Fred Kinver had finished his office work for the evening, then the Paper Man moved in and completed his own, burying it like a dog with his bone as before.

Soon he would have a second death to write about.

EARLIER that same evening, the day of the funeral, Jim and Val Humberstone had met in the kitchen, where Val now held sway. The Mongrel dog Bob had had an early walk and was now eating his supper at her feet. He had not noticed the absence of Kay Zeman. Out of sight, out of mind, was how he lived, even though everyone thought he might pine.

'Thanks, Jim. Behaved all right, did he?'

'Bob's always a good boy.' He patted Bob's head, Bob went on eating regardless, but he moved his face protectively closer to his food bowl. 'Wouldn't mind having him as my dog.'

'I'll remember that, Jim.' She pressed her head. 'Oh dear.'

'Are you all right, Miss Val?' He always called her that, he would have liked her a lot if she had not been so keenly focused on Leonard and Timmy Zeman.

'Got a bad cold, I'd like to take a drink to bed.'

'Whisky and lemon is good.'

'Yes.' Her eyes wandered to the tin of drinking chocolate on the side. Hot milky chocolate was more her style. Soothing, sweet. Some of those chocolate cakes that she loved. 'But I've got to go out, unluckily.'

'Well, don't bother then, Miss Val,' said Jim soothingly. Off to have a drink in St Luke's Mansions with the policeman. There wasn't much he didn't get to know about his employers in Feather Street. They were good talkers and quite often shouted, you only needed sharp ears and an accurate memory. He and the dogs were an essential part of the workings of Feather Street. He told the dogs everything, even Jumbo, who was a bastard but not to be blamed for what was not his fault, and thought more of them than the families. The Annecks, the Darbyshires, the Zemans, what were they but a lot of snobs?

He had picked up the whiff of alienation in the air, knew he did not like the police, nor the government, nor a lot of the people he saw around him, but he was not yet sure on which side of the great divide he stood, except he did not think it was with the Feather Street lot.

'No,' she sighed, 'I must go. I owe it to Timmy.'

'Owe Timmy, Miss Val?'

'Yes, you wouldn't understand.' She sighed again, and it turned into a cough. 'I must. There are some things we have to do, Jim.'

If she must go, she must, thought Jim. He agreed with her that some things had to be done. Like walking dogs, and delivering the milk. Having babies and dropping dead. He thought he knew about what you had to do as much as most... She didn't look up to it, though, she'd be better dealing with that cold.

Val said: 'Do I owe you anything?' He liked to be paid on time, as, who didn't?

'No, you paid me,' he reminded her. 'Before... before Mrs Zeman died.'

'Oh yes, so I did.' She might so easily have forgotten in the confusions of her aunt's sudden death and the funeral. What a beautiful face Jim had, she thought, like a Botticelli angel, at once loving, yet intellectual and withdrawn. No doubt, this look would not survive his adolescence, but he had it now. He was a good cook too, had some of her best recipes, it was amazing what people were. 'But there's this week. I'll just get my purse.'

'Don't worry, Miss Val.'

'Oh, I will. The weekend is coming, after all. You might be glad of it.'

She got her purse, and paid the boy, who nodded gravely.

'Goodbye, Jim.' She dragged herself up the stairs to get ready for her meeting with John Coffin. She had a new dress, but possibly the day of a family funeral was not the time to wear it.

Her bedroom was warm in the late afternoon sun which made pools of light on the dressing-table where the shiny dark mahogany showed up the dust of several days. Val sat down and saw herself in the glass.

'Poor old thing, look at you.' She picked up the hairbrush, but it felt too heavy to lift and her arm reluctant to do the service. 'It's only a summer cold, they are always the worst, although Leonard says that's nonsense. I'll have a hot drink and feel better.'

Not hot chocolate, she would have a cup of tea, and something to eat. With surprise, she realised that she had hardly eaten all day. Felicity had provided drinks and sandwiches after the funeral, but she hadn't touched a thing. She couldn't eat Felicity's food while thinking what she did. Tim hadn't eaten much either, poor lad, but then he had other worries.

The police had set up another interview, oh, politely, of course, but advised him to bring a solicitor. His father too, if he liked. They would be asking for body specimens. Everyone knew what that meant.

'I can help you, Tim,' she said to her reflection, 'but whether you will be pleased with me for doing it is more than I can say.'

Her reflection frowned back at her. 'I ought to pluck my eyebrows,' she told her face. 'I look heavy and dull today.' It was one of those days all women know when their faces do not belong to them.

STELLA PINERO was in the room and looking good. She was an actress and knew how to manage her face.

Even though he didn't want her in the room and wished she'd go away, Coffin liked the way she looked.

Of course she was there with a purpose, Stella usually was. She might act casually, but she was really walking in a straight line for what she wanted.

Coffin had got home eventually, after his detour round Elder Street. He had thought about viewing Feather Street but had decided Not Today, after all, Val Humberstone would be calling on him, and he wanted to be there. He sensed it was going to be important. The weekend was approaching, but that didn't mean much to him, these days.

Before he had the door closed behind him, Stella had rung the bell and was in before he could say Hello.

'I usually love seeing you, Stella, but tonight I am tired and need a shower and a drink. What is it you want? Haven't you got a play to produce?'

'In train. I'll pour you a drink.' She was wearing white trousers and a cream shirt. 'I need one myself.'

'Give me five minutes.' He disappeared into the bedroom.

Stella sank back in a chair with her drink. She knew from experience that five minutes could mean anything. Soon she heard water running in the shower.

'You hungry?' she called out. 'I've got Harry Beauchamp and Dick coming in for a meal. Max is sending round. Join us.'

'Thank you, I would, but you might remember that Val Humberstone is also coming round.'

'But of course I remember. I'm inviting her too. I'll just wait till she gets here, say Hello, invite her, and then take Harry and Dick tactfully away to check on the wine, they love thinking about wine, and she can talk. Plenty of food for us all, do her good to get out. I thought she looked terrible at the funeral. You weren't there, by the way.'

Stella got up and carried his drink in to the shower.

'Here, wait a minute, Stella,' he protested. 'Let me get something on.'

'I'm theatre, ducky, remember? I don't notice anything like that.' Or only when I choose to, she thought happily. Men were such prudes.

She took her drink back to the sitting-room, sipped it, then called out: 'Don't you want to know why I came before Val? I'm worried.'

Coffin appeared at the door, dressed and carrying his drink.

'I think I need police protection,' she said. 'Or the theatre does. Both of us, all of us. We've had more nasty messages painted on the wall. Threatening to burn us down this time, I think they mean business.'

'I doubt it.'

'If they burn us down, then they might burn your flat down too.'

'Now there is a thought,' said Coffin, sitting down and finishing his drink. 'That would upset Letty, her investment going up in smoke.'

'It wouldn't do much for me.' Stella stood up, tall and cross. 'You'd better take this seriously.'

'I do, Stella, I do.'

'You're not doing anything about it, though.'

'What I can.' How could he get across to her the complexities he faced? The hostility and suspicion from various groups, the steady pressure of organized pressure groups, and always, of course, the operations of the dirty tricks brigade. Some of the hostility and suspicion came from his own side, too.

'Not enough, though, I'll probably have to get beaten up or raped or something before you lot operate. I nearly caught the nasty lout that painted the last messages on the wall, but he ran off. He turned and showed his teeth at me like a dog. Horrid crooked yellow teeth, too.'

'What did you do?'

'I shouted Clean your teeth.'

In spite of himself, Coffin laughed. 'They'll never beat you, Stella.' He remembered something. It might suit him to meet Sir Harry. 'I'd like to have a word with Harry Beauchamp. He may have some useful photographs of Rope Alley.'

'Bloody policeman,' she said. Not entirely amiably. 'I don't believe you'd care if I did get raped or killed.'

It got under his skin. He gripped her wrist, hard, tight. 'Yes, Stella, bloody. Police work is bloody. Literally so quite often. It is bloody, terrible, frightful, frightening and unpleasant. You can feel cut off from the rest of the group you live in. You are cut off. I've shielded you from all that, Stella. You think you understand, but you don't.'

They were standing there, still confronting each other when the sound of Max's voice could be heard from the stairs. He seemed to be talking about Chicken Maryland.

'Not nice work, Stella.' Coffin dropped her arm. 'And it makes me not a nice man, remember that.'

'That's Max,' said Stella. She withdrew her arm, rubbing her wrist.

'Yes, that's Max.'

'Are you coming to eat?'

Hostility was still bristling between them.

'I've told you: I've got Val coming.'

'Leave a note.'

'I can't do that.'

From the stairs another voice had joined Max's, this one talking of chilled white wine.

'That's Harry,' said Stella. 'I know. Let's all have dinner right here.' And she darted towards the door, calling as she went.

I never learn, thought Coffin, she's done it again. Another party is assembling here.

He reached out an arm and stopped her. 'Wait a minute. I do take your alarms seriously, and I do mind very much the tensions that are building up. I'm doing what I can.'

Stella leaned forward and kissed him.

A soft voice from the open door, said: 'Sorry to interrupt, but there's a lot of food piling up on the stairs.'

Coffin drew away.

'Bring it down here, please. Sir Harry. We're eating here.'

Max and his youngest daughter, the one they called 'The Beauty' (and who had been very beautiful at fifteen but was steadily growing less beautiful with every year that passed, as is the way with some girls), carried in the heated containers. Max had but recently added this delivery-at-home service to his delicatessen, he was very anxious to make it a success because he hoped, when the big theatre was finally in operation, to do the catering for it. As it was, he provided sandwiches and quiches and cream layer cakes of great richness for the bar which was all the Theatre Workshop ran to at the moment.

He was extremely anxious to please Stella Pinero and John Coffin, both of them powerful figures in his world. From his point of view, Sir Harry was a joyful addition to his circle. A patron, indeed.

'Put the tray of garlic bread on the side, Bella.' Bella was the Beauty daughter. 'The salad on the table.' He rested a big covered dish on a tray on a side table. 'I brought plates and cutlery, Miss Pinero, I didn't know how you were placed for them ... Shall I lay the table?'

'No, I'll do it.' Stella was prancing around holding several bottles of white wine. She seemed enlivened by her quarrel with Coffin whereas he still felt bruised. He had noticed before that she always came out of an altercation in high spirits. Possibly it was all an act.

Stella was acting all the time. He had to consider that.

'The wine is chilled, no more freezing, please, or it will spoil. The salad is organic. Miss Goldstone said to me that unless all my fruit and vegetables are organic she will no longer eat with me.' He sighed. Life was difficult, the organic vegetables and salad did not look as neat, pretty and well matched as the old ones, but Lily Goldstone was another star in his heaven.

From the door, he said: 'And the chicken is free-range. Miss Goldstone says I must.'

'Why does everyone take so much notice of Lily Goldstone?' asked Sir Harry, as Max got himself and Beauty out of the room and he himself opened a bottle of wine. His friend Dick had crept quietly into the room and was effacing himself against the wall.

'Because she's Lily,' said Stella simply.

Lily Goldstone, a surpassing actress, an ardent lover (when the mood took her), and affectionate mother and daughter, was a keen campaigner for anything that took her eye. It might be anything. Naturally theatre matters got most of her attention, but other causes from battery chickens to mink coats and Mrs Thatcher might come the way of her attentions.

'She might be looking in later,' went on Stella. 'We have things to talk about. She's got a new name to put on The Black List and wants Equity to do something about it.'

The Black List was the tally of companies and producers who had let Equity members down. Usually by going bankrupt and not paying them. The list was long. It fluctuated. Names went on it, then came off, then went on again. There was a hard core of names that never seemed to get free, caught in a web of debt for ever. Everyone knew them. You cut your theatrical teeth on the names not to take work with. Didn't mean you didn't do it sometimes, though, in desperation and hope that this time it would be different.

'She's heard of a production company that engaged a whole cast, jugglers and all for a revival of *Kismet*, rehearsed for two weeks, played for another two in Bottingham Playhouse and never paid a penny... Second time it's done it, too. Change of name, of course. Fiesta Productions the first time and Happy Days the second time round. It was Billericay the first time. JoJo Bell was the Equity dep... Naturally she's indignant. She's got on to Lily.'

'Wasn't it silly of JoJo to join up?' Coffin knew JoJo Bell, she had played in an early production at the Theatre Workshop. JoJo had had a part in a long-running hospital series on TV and afterwards had seriously thought of taking a medical degree. She had fantasies about her medical prowess.

'We all do silly things sometimes, and she's found it hard to get work with that doctor-nurse image hanging over her. All she kept getting offered were medical parts or invalids, and not many of them. She needed the money, I expect.'

'I've taken some good photographs of this lovely lady,' said Sir Harry, who never minded praising himself, as he poured the wine. He seemed to have taken over as host, just as Stella was acting hostess, laying the table and telling everyone where they would sit. Tiddles, who had just come in through a roof window, looked morosely around. He didn't like a crowd, but he did like chicken and had developed a depraved taste for garlic bread. 'And also the Workshop's new production of *Cavalcade*. Lovely crowd scenes. The Master would have been pleased.' Stella looked gratified.

'He is pleased,' said Dick, who was a dogged and unusually open believer in the spirit world.

'Don't be a fool, Dick,' said Sir Harry lovingly.

Coffin sat back and sipped some wine. Val was going to walk into the middle of a party, and although it might be good for her, as Stella had said, it would surely put her off talking. He wanted to know what she had to say in private. Val struck him as a private person.

'When do you expect Val?' Stella had read his thoughts. 'Shall we wait? Shall I give her a ring?'

'Any minute now. And No to the two other questions.'

Then the telephone rang. He carried his portable telephone to the window and turned his face to listen quietly. 'Yes, of course. I quite understand. Tomorrow, then? Shall we say the morning? In my office. You know where to come?'

Val spoke again and Stella, observing him, thought his face changed, looked graver. 'Right, don't worry now. Tomorrow, then.'

'Val,' he said, turning back towards them. 'Doesn't feel up to coming tonight.'

Stella made a move towards the door. 'I'm going round there.'

He stopped her. 'Leave her.'

Chewing on a piece of Chicken Maryland, free-ranging and dead, he thought: A bit like Anna Mary Kinver, who had been free-ranging in her relationships and was now dead.

'Sir Harry,' he said. 'You took some photographs of Rope Alley. For publicity purposes.'

'Yes, I did.'

'Where were they taken from?'

'From the roof of the old Lead Works. I looked down on Rope Alley.'

'Can I see them?'

'Of course. Dick has a complete set of those photographs. Is it in connection with the murder of that girl?'

Coffin nodded. A piece of that free-range chicken had got stuck in his throat. He managed to cough it free. What a way to die, he thought, killed by a chunk of loose-living chicken.

'They were nearly all taken several days before the murder,' said Sir Harry gravely. 'Except for one or two. Not the best.'

'I know. I just want to see them. They might give me something.'

He had learnt from experience that you must take what chance offered you to start you thinking. These photographs might do that for him now.

AFTER THE MEAL the three of them walked round to the Lead Works Gallery while Stella went downstairs to her open apartment in St Luke's Mansions to talk to Lily Goldstone about Black Lists. Dick took them into his office, which was a neat little cubbyhole, very quiet and peaceful, and produced a folder.

Coffin concentrated on those taken on the day of the murder.

There were several photographs taken at different times of the day. One was clearly a bright morning, near noon, with well defined sharp shadows. A number of people had been caught walking in Rope Alley. Seen foreshortened as they were, not much detail could be made out. This wasn't what Sir Harry had been after, he had wanted what he called a bit of urban landscape.

There was a woman with a shopping-bag. She was walking towards the camera. A man in the distance, seen from the back. Another man leaning against the wall. A few other shadowy figures including a boy on a bike. The Alley had been busy that morning.

Another photograph taken in the late afternoon with longer shadows was quieter. A trousered figure at the end of the alley, another one seen just in profile, and a young woman with a child.

A third photograph had been taken at night with a special lens. Only two figures this time: a man walking away from the camera and another leaning against the wall again.

The leaning man could be Soloman Wild, it had the look of him. Blown up, the photograph might yield a more positive indication.

But it was the image of the other man on which Coffin put his finger.

'That one. I think he's the same man in all three pictures. Something about the way he holds himself. He must have gone up and down Rope Alley a lot.'

He turned to Harry Beauchamp. 'May I have these photographs, please? And the negatives?'

'Of course. Glad to help, aren't we, Dick?' His friend nodded, he was a man of few words.

Later that night Coffin took a stroll round the whole complex of buildings about the old St Luke's Church. He surveyed the work done on the church itself where the big theatre would go. It was little more than a hole in the ground at the moment, and looked a highly expensive one. He had to hope that Letty was not wasting her money. But probably not. She was already calling it the National Theatre of the New City.

He walked over to the more makeshift buildings of the Theatre Workshop where advance posters proclaimed the next production of *Cavalcade*.

He could see where slogans had been painted and then effaced by Stella. Faint shadows rested on the walls. Shadows of hostility.

He hated this reflection of the divisions in the population where he and his Force kept the peace. They were in the middle and the object of resentment and criticism from all sides and all ethnic groups.

From his upper windows in the tower he looked down upon the quiet streets with the river beyond. It looked so peaceful. He hoped it stayed that way.

Inside her ground-floor apartment in St Luke's Mansions, Stella checked all the locks on her doors and windows. She listened for a moment. It's a war, she thought.

But all was quiet. It was after midnight. Saturday.

# EIGHT

*Saturday night into Sunday, June 18*

STELLA LAY IN HER BED and looked at the ceiling. It was a hot night, muggy and damp with a torrid feeling which only London in high summer with no wind can achieve. She was too nervous to have a window open. She must have a metal grille fixed.

She shifted uneasily, trying to get cool. Under the sheet she was wearing only a thin silk nightgown but even that felt too much. She slipped it off and tossed it to the ground. Somehow her body still felt hotter than the sheets. Perhaps she should have kept the gown on. It was amazing how warm and sticky bare skin could feel.

She wondered how John Coffin was doing upstairs. It was probably cooler in his tower.

She tossed around, restless and nervous.

In all her life, which had included two marriages and numerous other alliances, no physical violence had ever been used against her. Certainly not in sexual attack.

She wondered what it felt like. What she would do? Would she see it coming and try to evade it, run away? That was the sensible thing to try for. She was fleet of foot and could run fast if she got the chance. Everyone said that was the best thing to do. Shout and run fast. She'd be able to shout, she knew how to use her voice.

But there might be nowhere to run. Trapped in a room, a passage, a dark corner, then you couldn't escape.

She'd fight, she knew herself well enough to know that as a truth. But she had never had to fight physically and would probably not be very good at it. She had to hope her teeth and nails would be sharp enough. She thought she could guarantee to leave a mark or two on her attacker.

But what would it really be like? This impact of one violent, hostile male body upon her own. The smell, there was bound to be a smell, all bodies had their own smell. There would be nothing pleasant about the attacker's smell. Drink, drugs, sweat, urine.

Stop that, Stella, she thought. Leave it.

She couldn't leave the subject. How would I feel if the worst happened?

She imagined the hands, the heat, the actual moment of penetration.

Unwelcome thoughts piled in.

And would you, in the end, enjoy it? Would your body simply say: This is what I was made for?

What a question to ask a woman, she thought, as she sat up in bed and piled the pillows behind her. You aren't supposed to ask that sort of thing. I won't answer.

But she did answer. No, she thought, the answer is No, because you'd be frightened, in pain, not ready.

But the body had its own rules, its own ideas. Nothing was certain.

I might cry if I go on thinking like this, she decided.

She went to the refrigerator and got herself some iced water, then carried it back to drink.

One thing was certain: if the worst happened, she would bear it better than one of the Feather Street ladies.

The moment she held that thought clearly in her head, she knew she was coming out of her bad mood, and feeling better.

You could always tell a Feather Street lady. They admitted it themselves. As well as Mary Anneck and Philippa Darbyshire, there was Alice Graham and Daisy Armour and Mrs Farmer (she had never got to know her first name, perhaps no one did) and Violetta Mason.

They all had the same walk, it was the way they put their feet down. Firmly and cleanly, as if they always knew the way. They didn't wear the same sort of clothes, but they always looked the same somehow.

They all went to the one hairdresser. Or didn't go at all. But it couldn't be that on its own. No, it was that they all thought they had a right to know.

To know what? she asked herself. To know what was necessary, of course.

Leaning back on her pillows, she began to feel interested. Well, she'd got the female side of Feather Street weighed up, but what about the men, no one mentioned them? That meant something. Then she felt amused, and then sleepy.

'Better now,' she told herself. 'All over.'

It was the sort of thing you said to a child after a bad dream, but it helped her.

She drifted off to sleep.

JOHN COFFIN was sleeping soundly in his tower. Night noises filtered up through the open window, but did not disturb him. He had his own private nightmares, but they were different from Stella's and centred more on civil riot and disturbance.

But sometimes he had a dark dream in which Stella was at the centre of this rampaging crowd, that she was pinned there, calling for help. The crowd wanted a scapegoat, a victim, and although it should be him, somehow it was Stella they had caught. And in this dark dream he failed to rescue Stella. He had woken, sweating yet shivering, from this dream more than once.

A church clock struck the hour, a cat called hopefully to another feline, a late aeroplane muttered across the sky to Heathrow. A night silence is made up of all sorts of noises, his brain accepted them and was not troubled.

But with dawn, one noise did get through to him. He turned over restlessly. It seemed to him he heard a dog whining.

Yet it was pretty far away, and presently it stopped. He had hardly stirred in his sleep.

But he remembered it when he woke up in full daylight, it was going to be another hot day, and he stood in his kitchen making a cup of that instant coffee that Stella so despised. She had bought him a special automatic coffee machine, but he never had time to use it.

And, as a matter of fact, he really liked this strong powdered sort he stirred up.

That dog in the night, what had it been upset about?

DEATH ALWAYS distressed a dog if it was forced to notice it. Bob, the mongrel, had not noticed the death of Kay Zeman because he had been carefully sheltered from it by Val and Jim Marsh, both of whom, in their different ways, had seen that his life went on as normal. Which was all a dog asked of life really.

But Bob could be frightened, and that night he had been frightened. He had noticed death.

FEATHER STREET AWOKE to the day slowly, and with care. They were usually stirred to life by the arrival of their milk, followed by the delivery of the newspapers and the post. When all three deliveries had been made, Feather Street got up and made breakfast.

Each household had its own favourite breakfast but there was a sort of similarity between them, as Stella would quickly have picked up. Milk was skimmed, but would have been unpasteurized if this had been procurable in London, bread was unbuttered, and fruit unsugared. Coffee, if taken, was carefully ground and filtered.

Being nearer to the whining Bob than John Coffin, the Feather Streeters had been more disturbed by him.

Leonard Zeman who was a heavy sleeper had heard nothing, but Felicity came down, fully dressed as always, and said: 'I think you ought to go over to Val's. There may be something wrong there.'

'What do you mean?'

'Didn't you hear the dog in the night? No, obviously you didn't. Well, there was a dog howling and I think it was Bob.'

They had a basement kitchen, always lit by artificial light and very clinical, so there was no looking out of the window, but it was what he wanted to do at that moment, to draw in some cool fresh air. He drank some chilled orange juice instead.

'Wake up, Len,' she said.

'How do you know it was Bob?'

'I didn't recognize his voice, if that's what you mean, but the howling was coming from that direction.'

'But it's stopped now.'

'He's a selfish old sod,' said Felicity. 'Once he'd got himself comfortable, he'd give up.' Arthur, her white peke, came and lay across her feet. Danger here, he was saying. 'It's not him I'm worried about.'

'You don't sound worried.' Nor did she, she sounded calm and quiet as if she was not surprised, as if this might even be something she had been expecting or even waiting for. Of course, she didn't like Val.

'I'll ignore that. Are you ready?'

'Yes, I'd better investigate.' The juice had woken him up. 'Are you coming too?'

'Of course.'

'This may be about nothing. Val can look after herself.' He was taking the keys of what had been his mother's house from the board where they hung for anyone to take as required.

'I'm glad you think so.'

'Where's Tim?'

'Still asleep. Tomorrow he goes for his interview with Superintendent Lane. I shall go with him, of course.'

'I think it would be better if I went.'

'As you wish,' she said. 'I just thought it might be easier for him if I went.'

'I'm close to Timmy,' said Leonard defensively. 'As close as anyone. I don't think one ought to keep bothering the lad.' He ignored the fact that the police, not to mention life itself, were about to bother Timmy in a substantial way.

'I don't think anyone is very close to Tim,' said his mother. 'Not at the moment, poor lad.' She led the way down the garden and along what they called the dog walk. A gap in the hedge would, by skirting the Anneck house, bring them to the other Zeman house. 'I think he's in a state of clinical shock. We really ought to get him looked at. Lieberman's good. He might be the man to go to.'

'My God, you can be cold sometimes, Fe.'

'Oh no, not cold at all.'

Felicity was not a Feather Street lady, you could tell it by her kitchen, by the way she walked. This was perhaps why she was not liked by the other ladies. They felt she was a different sort of animal.

'Lieberman, though. So that's what you think of Timmy. That would please the police, if we walk in there with Timmy in the care of an expert in criminal psychology. They'd probably get the handcuffs out straight away.'

'Lieberman has other interests,' said Felicity coolly. 'And Timmy has other problems. You may not choose to call them that, but I think he does.'

When you approached this Zeman house from the back you saw how badly it needed painting, Leonard, who was his mother's executor, knew that she had left it to Val for her lifetime and then to Timmy. Val knew this, and probably Tim too. The unwritten provision was that with the house went Bob the dog.

Everything was very quiet, but Val never got up early.

'Shall we go in at the back?'

'We can't just burst in,' said Leonard.

'Val won't be too surprised if she sees you, will she?' said Felicity drily. 'I mean it won't be exactly the first time.'

Leonard ignored this. 'I'll ring the bell.'

'No one ever answers that backdoor bell. I can't think when anyone ever rang it. My goodness, there isn't a tradesmen's entrance these days.'

They were standing arguing in the garden.

Leonard got the keys out of his pocket and opened the back door. 'Val, you there? Val?'

No answer.

He went through the kitchen, where there were signs that Val had made herself a drink at one point, there was the open tea-caddy and the tin of biscuits. She had left the bottle of milk outside the refrigerator; in the hot night it had gone sour and looked solid.

In the sitting-room, Bob was in his basket, sleeping heavily, he gave little snorting snores every so often.

'Told you he'd be asleep,' said Felicity. 'But where's Val?'

'She's upstairs asleep, I expect,' said Leonard. 'We shall look fools.'

'But why doesn't she answer?'

Felicity went to the bottom of the stairs. 'Val, are you there? It's Felicity.'

She started to move up the stairs, but Leonard drew her back. 'Wait. Let me.'

Felicity halted. She was a doctor too, but if there was anything wrong, then probably Val would prefer Leonard to find her. In this restraint Felicity was unlike the Feather Street ladies, not one of whom would have hesitated to go bounding up the stairs to see what was what.

She stood at the bottom of the stairs, looking at her hands, capable, well scrubbed, good hands. Hands which obeyed her behest, whatever she told them to do.

Leonard came to the top of the stairs. 'Fe... Come up.' His speech was unsteady, as if he could not breathe.

Felicity walked up the stairs slowly, not hurrying.

In the back bedroom which had always been hers, Val was lying on the bed on her side, her face buried in the pillows. She had been sick.

On a tray by the bed was a small teapot with a cup and saucer. A plate, empty except for chocolate-coloured crumbs, was on the floor, as if Val had knocked it from the table.

Her body was still warm, but she was not breathing.

Felicity drew away from the bed.

'Shall we try resuscitation?'

'No.' Leonard was still having difficulty with his breathing. 'It's been too long. If we did bring her back, the brain would be gone. There would be nothing there.' He drew a bedcover over Val's face. 'She's not there now.'

Felicity picked up the plate and put it on the table.

Leonard was still looking at the bed. 'There'll have to be an inquest this time.'

'Why do you say that?' A strange thing to say. This time? When was last time? She was aware she should not have asked. But some questions just pop out.

'I'm not sure. At all events I can't give a death certificate. She's not my patient. Not even in our practice.'

Of course not, thought Felicity, they would be too wise to mix patient and lover relationships.

'She's under Jeff Green at the Elmgate Centre. I don't know what he's been prescribing. If anything.' It was hateful to talk about darling Val in this way, as if she had not been a person he loved, but professional training helped.

'I'll 'phone him for you, shall I?'

'No, I'll do it myself. Better that way.' He looked at the plate. 'Not sure if you ought to have touched that plate.'

'Why?'

'The police...' He didn't finish the sentence. 'It depends on what Jeff Green says, but I think it's something we've got to face.'

They went down to the kitchen together. The telephone was in the hall; Kay Zeman stuck to that old-fashioned placing when everyone else had them all over the place, and even in a pocket.

Leonard started to dial the Elmgate Health Centre and his wife went through the kitchen.

'Where's the dog?' he called, telephone in his hand.

'Asleep in his basket.'

Bob was in his basket, still asleep, still breathing heavily, but now irregularly in bursts.

'Cheyne-Stokes breathing,' recorded Felicity absently, without thinking much, her mind still on Val and the telephone call Leonard was making and what might follow.

Then she looked at the dog, knelt down by him, and touched his nose. He did not stir. He was too deeply asleep.

She thought: It wasn't for Val he was howling, but for himself. Bob thought he was going to die.

# NINE

*Tuesday, June 20*

IN NO TIME AT ALL, the Paper Man had his message in to John Coffin. He could have written it any time, but he must have posted it on the Monday because Coffin got it the next day. So did Inspector Archie Young, so did Stella Pinero. The network was widening.

It was one of his now usual letters in style and presentation.

> *Told you there would be a second death, didn't I?*
> *The Paper Man.*

He was actually calling himself that now. Somewhere he had picked up the name, or gone out looking for it, anyway. It was a name he liked. It suited him, what he was, or pretended to be. A name you could hide behind.

The Paper Man began to meditate on the next steps in his campaign. It was a campaign. He had never served in any army so the phrase had no military connections for him, but it sounded aggressive, and hostile and punitive. All of which he intended to be.

Stella didn't know what to make of her letter, except that she didn't like it. Nasty associations began to brew up in her mind with the lout with the teeth. She could not forget him, because she had a horrible feeling he meant to remember her.

Mrs Kinver had come back to work in the Theatre Workshop, moving around quietly but doing her job as well as ever.

What a nice woman, Stella thought, watching her ironing a blouse. Only reflecting thoughtfully that it was Lily Goldstone's blouse, not one of her own. Trust Lily to get in on the act and Mrs Kinver to do a favour. Of course, Lily would pay her, no doubt about that, but Mrs Kinver would have done it in any case. She was a fan of Lily's and went to all her plays, even those sternly intellectual ones that Lily delighted in and hardly anyone enjoyed. (Although never admitting it openly. Lucid, they would say; a revealing theatrical appearance which left this critic stunned.)

Stella watched the iron go back and forth. You can see she's unhappy but she isn't letting it be a nuisance to other people.

She herself felt tense and unhappy. She had gone to bed on Saturday night full of fears about her own safety. Life seemed so precarious, civilized ways so threatened. Sunday morning had dawned quietly, with coffee in bed and the newspapers to read. Then the telephone had rung with the news that Val was dead. Even now she had hardly taken it in, but the shock was there.

Neither of the two women spoke to each other of Anna Mary or the murder investigation which was going on all around them. Stella had shown her sympathy on a much earlier occasion and she understood that Mrs Kinver wanted to get on with her grief in her own way, not be dug up every so often to see how she was getting on. They both knew that Tim Zeman had been back in the police's hands, and had submitted to having blood and other specimens taken. The word was he was out again, still uncharged.

It was mid-afternoon on a fine Tuesday. Tuesday was the day Mrs Kinver always did the ironing and she was sticking to the rules.

The ironing done, she usually had a quiet cup of tea, then went home, to come back to the theatre as required. Tuesday was not a matinée day.

'Like a cup, Miss Pinero?' Mrs Kinver made the offer in a kindly spirit. Stella was hanging about, not settling to any of the work she had in front of her, scripts to read, bills to check, letters to write.

'Please.' They sat down together in a friendly way at the kitchen table. When Letty Bingham, Coffin's sister and ultimate owner of the freehold of these flats, had planned the kitchen, she had said to Stella: 'You won't need a table, no one has a kitchen table now,' but Stella had replied firmly that she had always had a kitchen table and she meant to have one now, and she trotted out to Peter Jones and bought a beauty. Pale marble with iron legs, not very comfortable to sit at, as it turned out, but lovely to see.

Stella drank her tea with thirst.

'Another cup, Miss Pinero?'

For answer, Stella pushed her cup forward.

'You don't look well, miss.'

'I'm still getting over Val Humberstone dying like that.' If it was tactless to talk about death to Mrs Kinver, it would be even more tactless to falsely deny the shock of Val's going. It was one death too many. 'It was so unexpected.'

'Missed her aunt, poor lady.'

'Oh, but Val didn't . . .' Stella started, then stopped. Didn't kill herself, she had been going to say, but how did she know? She had no idea what had caused Val's death. She had taken something, either by accident or design, because Bob had had some too. Val would never have poisoned Bob. But how did you know?

'I didn't mean that,' said Mrs Kinver. 'Not that she killed herself. We'd know that by now, wouldn't we? And they haven't said.' The mysterious They who often figured in Mrs Kinver's conversation were both omniscient and omnipotent but also anonymous. Just one aspect of the powers that operated on her life and over whom she had no control. She had never heard of Kafka but would have recognized a fellow spirit. This time she meant the police, but it might have been the government or the National Health Service. All were 'They'. 'No, I just meant if she was ill and perhaps didn't even know it, then her aunt dying might have taken away that last little bit of energy she needed. Do they know the cause? Her heart, was it?'

'I don't know what Val died of. I don't think anyone knows yet.' There was going to be a post-mortem and then, necessarily, an inquest, but she would not mention that to Mrs Kinver.

Mrs Kinver shook her head regretfully. 'We're not lucky round here, are we? The milkman's boy, young Jim Marsh, told me the little dog was ill too.'

'Bob's all right,' said Stella. He was at present living with her. No one else seemed to want him. She wasn't sure if she did, and Tiddles certainly didn't, that wily animal had moved in permanently with John Coffin, who didn't know it yet but would soon realize that this was forever and no passing visit.

'Such a nice lady too,' went on Mrs Kinver. 'She should have got away.'

It wasn't clear what she meant by this remark, although Stella could guess. Got away before her fate, whatever it was to be, caught up with her. An appointment in Samarra, she thought. You can't run from what gets there before you.

'You ought to go away on holiday yourself,' she said. 'Later on.'

An unspoken dialogue was going on between them. What Stella meant was: After the murderer has been caught.

'Depends,' said Mrs Kinver. 'You never know, do you?'

What she meant was: If he ever is caught.

'I'm worried about Fred, Miss Pinero.' She looked down at her cup. She shook her head. 'Not himself.'

In their private dialogue this meant he was, in fact, behaving in a highly abnormal fashion.

Not surprising, thought Stella, she did not feel normal herself. This wasn't how life should be. 'Seen the doctor?'

Mrs Kinver shook her head.

Not physically ill then, more mental. And who could blame him? It was amazing how Mrs Kinver was holding together. A strong woman.

'I'm afraid he might do something.'

Something violent, she meant. But to himself or to others? Probably she did not know. Stella took this confidence seriously. Something would have to be done.

'Oh, he wouldn't,' said Stella.

'No, I don't suppose so, he's a gentle man, my Fred. But I feel better now I've had a cup of tea and talked to you. I can see I'm being a silly woman. Now I'll wash things up. That is, if you've finished.'

'I'll have another cup,' said Stella mechanically. Certain things in this conversation needed thinking over, and had been uttered so that she should think about them.

'Do you want me in this evening?' Mrs Kinver was running the water into the bowl; there was a dish-washing machine, but she never used it. Under running water and then a good dry with a clean cloth was so much better. She acted as dresser to Stella in the theatre, if needed.

'If you can manage it. It's a costume run-through, later tonight, after the show, for *Cavalcade*.'

Mrs Kinver's face lit up. 'I'll love it. Give me a real lift, it will.'

'We could do with Fred giving a hand backstage if you think he's up to it.'

'Do him all the good in the world, Miss Pinero. I'll see he does.'

Stella went through to her bedroom to prepare herself for her evening's work. She hadn't a big part in the present production, since she had only just come out of a West End show, nor was she its director (that honour had gone to a young graduate from the University Drama Department who had done a great job), but one or two things had gone awry lately and they were going to have a conference about it.

She put on some clean white cotton trousers and a new shirt of red silk. She felt she was divided into two people. One person was the practical and accomplished actress who was driving forward with all her ambitions for the Theatre Workshop and, incidentally, for herself. That person was pragmatic and optimistic.

But there was this other person who was shivering inside, who had premonitions of bad things to come, who believed in evil.

Bob was asleep in the middle of her bed, his round form covered in rough ginger and white fur making a dent in the antique lace cover.

Trying it on, thought Stella. He'd have to learn better than that. She pulled at his collar. 'Off, boy.'

Bob gave a soft growl, but Stella was not intimidated. 'If you want to live with me, and frankly, I don't fancy the prospect, we will have to come to terms. Off the bed.'

Bob, no fool when it suited him not to be, slid off the bed, leaving behind him on the white lace a nicely grubby and ginger patch.

When Stella had gone to her meeting, he walked slowly round her flat, investigating it. She had left a bowl of water and a dish of food out for him, so he dealt with these first, then he took another look round. Not his idea of a good home, no cosy nooks, not many soft spots for a dog to rest. The food was decent, though, and appreciated now he was beginning to feel more himself. It would do. But he missed the garden. He had forgotten Val, forgotten Mrs Zeman, forgotten Jim Marsh, but he would remember him as soon as he saw his face.

He was not used to the noises of this place; there were plenty of them, feet coming lightly but firmly down some stairs nearby, the sounds of voices through the open window, a distant noise of traffic, together with all the creaking and whisperings of an old building.

He thought he heard someone at the door. Being a dog who took his duties seriously, he gave a low, firm growl.

Heavy tread. A man's. Probably friendly. Better not run any risks. He gave another long growl.

Whoever it was went away.

IT WAS JOHN COFFIN the other side of the door, his tread that Bob had heard, Coffin he had growled at.

Stella's got a watchdog now, Coffin thought as he turned away. I wasn't really going to call, just look in and see how she was.

Perhaps he had had more in his mind than that simple quest; he had wanted to see Stella for himself. But in addition he had meant to ask her to come with him round the Zeman house in Feather Street where Val Humberstone had died. Lived and died.

He was puzzled about that death, they all were, there was considerable perturbation in the police team. Did it have any connection with the death of Anna Mary Kinver? If so, what, and how?

It was also causing more troubles in the neighbour-hood. He could sense the tension rising. Nor was it imagination, he had solid reason. Feather Street was clogged with people trying to get a look at the Zeman house. A brick had been thrown through Leonard Zeman's office window, and a wall at the bottom of Feather Street had been daubed with the word MUR-DERERS.

All this activity was unreasonable and illogical, but threatening.

Also, he had received advance information that the local newspaper would be launching a hostile editorial at him.

In addition, a BBC research team had arrived in the neighbourhood to interview and photograph the inhabitants. He did not know the exact nature of the programme being prepared, but he could guess. Somewhere in it there would be criticism of the police.

All in all, the death of Val Humberstone spelt trouble for the Chief Commander and his police force in the Second City of London.

He wanted desperately to know if Val Humberstone had died naturally or killed herself. Or been killed.

He wanted her to have died naturally but somehow he did not think she had.

The letter from the Paper Man seemed to suggest otherwise. If so, and Val's death was not just a coincidence, how did the writer of the letter (whoever he or she was) know what was going to happen?

The odds against Val Humberstone having died naturally were shortening.

Well, the post-mortem might show how Val Humberstone had died. Not that they always did, he reflected gloomily, sometimes you didn't get an answer. It wasn't magic, a post-mortem, you were in the hands of the scientists and they were cautious people.

He had been told who was doing this post-mortem and he knew that Dr Angela Livingstone was one of the slow and careful ones.

But he wanted to go round the Zeman house and he wanted to go with Stella, because Stella had had a letter from the Paper Man and that must mean something. That particular letter had been handed over to Inspector Archie Young, who had his experts working on it. The first judgement seemed to be that it was alike in wording to that which had come to John Coffin, and similar in all respects in the way it was put together. The letters had probably been cut from the same source at the same time. The slightly shiny paper suggested a quality newspaper or magazine.

Sir Harry Beauchamp was coming through the narrow passage that led between St Luke's Mansions and the Theatre Workshop. He was accompanied by his assistant who was carrying all the bags. Sir Harry himself was burdened with nothing more than a copy of *Vogue* under his arm, American edition.

'Ructions going on in there,' he said, giving a nod in the direction of the Workshop offices. 'Nothing like actors for quarrelling. Artists are peace itself by comparison. Well, they don't meet together so often, I suppose. A fat young man they called the Equity dep was tearing into Stella about something he called Clause Eighteen B. However, she was holding up nicely.'

'Oh, she would do.'

'Glad to see you, would have called anyway. Have you got anything out of those photographs yet?'

'Not yet.'

'I've got some blow-ups for you. Might not help. Don't give more detail, but these are slightly different shots. There you are.' He handed a packet over. 'Worth a look. Hope you get something out of them.'

Coffin accepted them. 'I'm grateful for them. I'll pass them on to the investigating team.' Having a look first himself, of course.

Then he went to the house in Feather Street where Val Humberstone had died. It had been left exactly as when Leonard and Felicity had walked in and found her. A quick survey had been made by a police detective, but they were waiting now for the post-mortem report. If it was natural death, then that was the end of it. If not, well . . .

The house was very still and quiet and stuffy. Smelt of the living, with just a faint whiff of death.

Coffin looked round the kitchen, then went up to the bedroom where the bedclothes were still in disarray.

On the bed table was the plate which Felicity had put there. The tea-tray was still there, but the teapot and the teacup had been taken away.

The plate except for a few crumbs had a well polished surface. An animal's tongue could give it a clean look like that, Coffin decided. Bob and Val had shared some food in that room, and both had suffered.

He took one last look round the house before leaving.

He got to his parking place behind the new police building just in time to see Archie Young driving slowly past it, giving it a loving look, measuring himself for it. Dreaming: That'll be mine one day.

Coffin knew the look, had had it himself in the past. Young would probably make it. He had that way with him, but his day was not yet.

'Wait a minute,' Coffin said, getting out the car. 'Want a word. Got something for you.' He handed over the packet of photographs that Sir Harry had given him. 'Bit more material from Sir Harry. Get yourself copies, then let me have these back.'

'Right, sir.'

Young looked bright and cheerful, although he had already done a hard day's work and was still at it as evening came on, a twenty-hour day this was going to be, but he never tired. He was a stocky man for his size, with a thatch of fair hair which was always untidy.

He looked at Coffin, seeing him, just for a moment, not as the Boss, or the Old Man, or WALKER, but as a man you might meet in a pub like anyone else. Tall, going grey, but not losing his hair, bright blue eyes, quite formidable when he concentrated on you. Kind, possibly ruthless all the same. Decent, he thought. Someone you could work for.

'Something to tell you, sir. Going to get the Paper Man letters in the press. Local and national papers. Superintendent Lane's idea, sir. Thinks it might flush out something.'

'Worth trying,' nodded Coffin. And typical of Paul Lane, never averse to a bit of publicity.

'You're working late, sir.' Young allowed himself the little friendliness, thinking that Coffin was not the sort to pull rank, and also not reluctant to draw attention to the fact that he himself was still at it.

'I had to come back for something.'

In his office, Coffin went to the machine that recorded his messages, found the relevant tape and played over the original telephone call from Val Humberstone asking for a meeting.

Nothing there, he thought, but tension in her voice. But all the same there is something I want to think about, something that nags at me.

He sat down and let his mind run over what she had said when she put off that appointment. He had covered up his alarm when he turned back into the room with Stella and Sir Harry and the ever-present Dick, but it had worried him.

Not the message itself.

I was probably the last person to talk to her, he thought. And her voice was wrong.

Yes, that was what worried me. On that second call there was something different about her voice.

And there was something wrong with her breathing.

Get on with it, Dr Angela Livingstone, he thought. Let me know what you've found.

# TEN

*Wednesday to Friday, June 21-23, with a retro-spective look at Tuesday again when Tim Zeman was interviewed*

IN THE RELATIVELY SMALL, new CID unit that was still in the process of building itself up, knowledge about different cases was freely passed around, and would have been even if the names Kinver and Zeman were not irretrievably twined in and out of each other. One case, two cases, who knew?

Science was meant to help, but had so far not spoken.

Superintendent Paul Lane said that Dr Angela Livingstone, the pathologist engaged in the post-mortem on Val Humberstone, was a smart girl and a thoroughly reliable worker, but a bit reserved; Inspector Archie Young said she was absolutely brilliant, a friend of his wife and had been at Cambridge with her. From which the Chief Commander of the Force they worked in, John Coffin, deduced that Paul Lane, who was a bit of a womanizer (in a nice way, people said), had made an advance to Angela and been rejected and that Archie Young hadn't thought of such a thing. So he said Good, he was glad to hear all that, but the trouble was she was very slow, and couldn't she be hurried up a bit? He wondered if he ought to mention that Val Humberstone's breathing had sounded abnormal, but in his experience scientists did not welcome lay help.

Paul Lane agreed to put pressure on. 'But what I'm interested in is the genetic fingerprint of the Zeman boy to see if it matches with that of the killer.' As found in the secretions on Anna Mary Kinver's body. 'If it does, then we've got him and no argument about it.'

They were not pleased, therefore, when on one and the same day the scientists checking the body secretions in question pointed out that they would have to be patient, these things took time, and Dr Angela Livingstone, instead of sending in her report, suggested she be allowed to examine the body of Mrs Kay Zeman, now some two weeks deceased.

It meant she had some clues to what had killed Val Humberstone, but she was not yet confident enough to say what. No one liked this, the news was kept quiet. Leathergate and Spinnergate were full of rumours.

There were too many bodies around. As well as the Zemans, an accident between a lorry and a bus crowded with schoolchildren had killed three seven-year-olds and a teacher. In addition, on that same morning a man had been found dead in the gutter outside the Spinnergate Tube Station. Mimsie Marker had found the body as she set up her newspaper stall just as the first trains of the day started to roll. She said he was a well-known gay character and to her mind he had died from a heart attack brought on by drink, and by what she tactfully called 'overdoing it'. Mimsie was almost certainly right, but it was one more cadaver.

The body of Anna Mary Kinver was still in the police mortuary. A brief and formal inquest had been held and then adjourned at the request of the police. It was hard on her parents, everyone agreed, especially those who had seen Fred Kinver lately, but there was no doing anything about it.

Local feeling was toughening about Timmy Zeman. The story was that he had killed Anna Mary Kinver, and his grandmother and Val Humberstone had known something that had incriminated him, so he was rubbing them out too. One by one. No coincidence, these two deaths, was the judgement. No testimony about body secretions and genetic fingerprinting was necessary for them, they knew the answer: Tim Zeman.

Whether John Coffin, Archie Young and Paul Lane liked it or not (and they didn't like it), the Zeman deaths were rapidly becoming part of the same problem with Anna Mary Kinver.

It was an added and unwelcome complication to Lane and Young that their boss was personally involved and taking what they felt to be an over-close and over-active interest in the case.

'I just wish he'd get off our backs,' said Superintendent Paul Lane, knowing full well from years of knowing Coffin that he wouldn't. 'Trouble is, he still thinks he's a working copper, and he isn't. Not any more. He's an executive running a large business, and crime detection is only a part of it.'

Archie Young preserved a tactful silence. He was on the sharper end of John Coffin's attention, getting the messages, questions, and demands and returning the answers, but he could do something for himself in the contact with WALKER.

John Coffin himself recognized the truth of the criticism which Paul Lane had not put into words yet had got across, but what Lane did not recognize was that emotions were involved which would not let him go.

It wasn't Stella, although being close to her always stirred things up; it was because of that case at the beginning of his career when he had walked upon, literally stumbled upon, the hands of a young girl who had been raped and murdered. That girl had been killed by her young lover.

Coffin admitted this prejudiced him against Timmy Zeman, which was why he had to see that justice be done.

Officially he had not met Tim Zeman, but he knew what the boy looked like because he had seen him at the theatre with his parents. He was tall like his mother with her eyes and bone structure, but he had his father's gentle manner. A boy with a sensitive expression, which might or might not mean a sensitive soul. You couldn't tell. He had known a murderer with a face like a Botticelli angel, and a saint with a broken nose. Tim looked intelligent, and coming from the family he did, then he probably was. Heredity and genetics did count for something.

Coffin let a day pass while he got on with other business. There was plenty of it. Sometimes he felt he might close his eyes on a peaceful dockside London one day, then wake up the next morning to find it was ablaze like Beirut. Or he'd be out to dinner somewhere and someone would ring up and say: You've got a riot in your area. He had to hope he would have been told before it got to that, but he couldn't count on it.

Public order, crowd psychology, were words he heard too often. The trouble was that the faces here were anonymous, and in the end crime was deeply personal. It was the death of your wife, your daughter, your son, even your neighbour, that gave you pain.

Thus he turned back to Timmy Zeman and Anna Mary Kinver.

He had taken the trouble to get the tapes of all the interviews the boy had had with Archie Young and Paul Lane, separately and together, they played it both ways. One of them went out, the other came back; one of them was good-humoured, the other threatening.

No doubt the boy had been confused, he was meant to be, to be thrown off his balance, ready to talk and make admissions.

However, he had made no admissions. At the first interview, his voice had sounded youthfully arrogant to begin with, then nervous, and finally frightened.

In successive interviews he had steadied, he had courage, but he had sounded cautious and tired.

Yes, he had admired Anna Mary very much. She was beautiful and nice to be with. Yes, very popular, everyone loved her.

Asked if he had loved her, he had said, 'No.' Very quiet on this, not saying much.

'So what about the poems?'

Yes, he had written those, but they were not specifically to her. Just love poems. Things he was writing. She was a good judge, he valued what she thought of them.

'So you are a poet?' It was Archie Young's voice.

Yes, he thought he might be, came the answer. It was what he wanted to be.

Silence for a bit then. Coffin could hear the shuffle of papers and the offer of a cup of tea which was accepted.

Sensible fellow, Coffin thought. Play for time, keep calm.

The boy seemed to be keeping calm, but you could hear the tension sharpening and making shrill his voice. Normally, he probably had a pleasant baritone. An educated boy, he spoke well.

After the tea, Paul Lane had put in his question:

'You may not have loved Anna Mary but you probably fancied her. You admit she was an attractive girl. Did you make love to her?'

'No.' A short and quiet response.

'Not ever?'

Again: 'No.'

This time it was a mumble, as though the boy had his head down on his chest.

'Perhaps you tried and were repulsed?'

'No. It wasn't like that.'

'But she was sexually experienced, you knew that?'

She had had lovers, the physical signs were there.

That would not please Fred Kinver. But the stories had already got about.

A bit of silence. Young, for it was he who now took it up after Lane, now pressed the question: 'Did you know?'

'I might have done.'

A juvenile answer, Coffin thought, not worthy of a boy who had shown himself intelligent.

But it highlighted the area, of sexuality, whether his own or hers, where he was sensitive and vulnerable. Or possibly guilty.

Archie Young then took up another tack: Where had he been on the night of the murder?

'I was away.'

'It wasn't far away, though, was it?'

'The other side of London, out towards Bromley.'

'And you could have got back? You had transport?'

'I had my motorbike. But my friends would have missed me.'

'But would they? My information is that there was a bit of a family crisis there, and you disappeared while they sorted themselves out.'

The boy was on the defensive now. 'There was a quarrel. My friend's parents started on at each other. I went to sit in the park while they got it over. I knew they would, they often fight but they make it up. When I thought it was right, then I went back.'

'Which park was that?'

'I don't know the name.'

'Anyone talk to you there? Anyone who will remember seeing you?'

'Shouldn't think so. I sat on a bench and read a book.'

'For hours? I believe you were gone some time?'

'I might have gone and had a Chinese.'

'Where?'

'Oh, I don't know, somewhere local. I don't remember.'

The thing was, Coffin thought, he might have done just that.

Or he might be guilty.

But there was an area of sensitivity here which needed to be explored.

The interrogation did not end at this point. Superintendent Lane, assisted by Archie Young, took Tim Zeman over all the ground again. Asking virtually the same questions, wording them a bit differently, placing them in another context as far as he could, using the usual tricks to try and trip him up.

The interview was interrupted at various points, Tim being left on his own except for a uniformed constable. No doubt the boy tried to talk to this young man, probably near his own age. But this was not recorded.

He would not have put it past Archie Young to have been running a private tape of his own to check on the times when the boy might relax his guard, but such tapes, supposing them to exist, would not be shown to the boss.

Coffin stopped the tape and went to the window of his office to look out. Night was coming on, but it was a light, pale summer night with a rising moon.

He had had a busy day, with several committees, a session with the local MP in the House of Commons, and a public meeting with an address to make. There were files and tapes on his desk, other cases, other problems, but he chose to stay with this one. It might be the most crucial of all.

He knew that Felicity Zeman had been in the building most of the day, although not in the room with her son. She had been joined towards the end of the day by Leonard Zeman.

He switched the tape back on again.

Another repetition of more or less the same set of questions to which Tim Zeman kept his answers in line with what he had already said. But he was tiring.

'Did you remove and take away one of Anna Mary's shoes?'

'No, I didn't.'

'Someone did. And we've never found it.'

'Not me. I'm not a shoe fetishist.'

'I never suggested you were. But you might have had other reasons, the shoe might have had your fingerprints on it.'

'I've told you: I wasn't there.'

Then Paul Lane slipped in his surprise: 'What would you say if I told you that I had a witness who places you in Spinnergate and near to Rope Alley on that evening?'

Coffin felt a shock of surprise.

There was silence from Tim Zeman.

Lane went on: 'A woman at the disco who knows you well. She works there.'

Silence still from the boy.

'You were wearing a hat and dark spectacles, but she recognized you.'

This had the ring of truth to it.

Tim collapsed. For a moment more the silence continued, then, in a choked voice, came the admission:

'Yes, I was there. I did ride back. But not to see Anna Mary. I never did see her. I never killed her.'

He would not say whom he was hoping to meet, or where.

A little later, very quietly, possibly in tears, Tim agreed to have any necessary tests made by the police surgeons, and to provide any specimens required. He asked for one of his parents to be present at the examination, and to this Superintendent Lane agreed.

Coffin switched off the tape.

You pulled a fast one there, Paul, he thought, but it worked.

On the whole, he was surprised that Lane had let the boy go that night, as he had done. But possibly they had had some forewarning that Dr Livingstone was going to ask to dig up his grandmother and wondered what poisoned broth was being brewed.

With the tapes had come a plastic folder containing the blow-ups of Sir Harry's photographs of Rope Alley at night.

He spread them around him on the desk. There was Rope Alley in the shadows of that dusky May night which had been moonless and overcast. One solitary street light had illuminated it. He could see the figure of the girl whom they had identified possibly, just possibly, as Anna Mary.

And there was the man to whom she might or might not be advancing with open hands. Coffin thought she looked as if she was doing that, but would not stake his life on it.

The male figure reminded him of something, he was looking at a round, tight little bottom.

What was the thought floating at the back of his mind, unable to surface? Push it back, leave it, and see what happens, experience told him. But it nagged.

He thought he might have a session with Solomon Wild, now undergoing therapy in a local clinic under police supervision. He was said to 'be coming round', although it was admitted on all sides he would never be totally normal. But he had been in Rope Alley and probably knew more than he was saying.

Coffin sat down thoughtfully. He got back to other work, but the problem stayed with him like an ache that would not be eased. He was uncomfortable, yet he hardly knew why.

He did not like the way this case was shaping. It had an ugly feel to it.

So this was how Coffin felt about the case at this point. Puzzled, sceptical, quite sure that there was something underground that was gradually pushing itself upward.

The Paper Man, on the other hand, although not privy to the evidence on the tapes, or to the photographs, felt that things were going just right.

•

TWO DAYS PASSED quietly enough. Fred Kinver was sleeping badly again. His wife knew that he got up at night and went walking. He still locked her in, but she had her own keys now. She had thought of getting up and following him, but she was too frightened. He was not a violent man, or never had been, but she was beginning to wonder what he was capable of just now. He seemed at his worst in the morning and in the middle of the night. During the day, he had gone back to doing odd jobs around the theatre for Stella Pinero, and running errands for John Dibbin, the local vet, who was doing a bit more drinking these days than was good for him or his practice. There was certainly a rivalry here between Fred and young Marsh, they were not friends and never would be, but managed to work together because they both liked animals, better than humans, anyway. Fred on the whole preferred cats, and Jim liked dogs.

Rehearsals for *Cavalcade* continued peacefully. It was going to be a good summer season. A whole troupe of locals had been recruited for the crowd scenes, which Stella felt must be right for public relations. She kept a wary eye open for the lad she called Teeth, but he was not seen and had not auditioned for a part. Not a would-be actor, obviously.

The slogans had duly been painted back on two outer walls of the Theatre Workshop complex, appearing overnight. YUPPIES FUCK OFF was the message this time, hastily removed but not before everyone had seen it.

The next morning the message just said: SHIT.

Lily Goldstone, coming in early for reasons of her own, but probably connected with her love-life, saw it and dealt with it.

She cleaned off the S and just left HIT, large and clear.

'Win by seeming to lose,' she said with a giggle. 'That's what the police say.' Surely her new lover could not be a copper?

Just occasionally, as on that Friday morning, a little frisson of terror, sheer terror, passed over Stella, but she dismissed it as nerves, and certainly told no one.

The Feather Street ladies, agreeing with each other for once, had postponed for a week a committee meeting about arrangements for a charity performance at the theatre in which Val had been deeply involved, and settled instead for a coffee session at Councillor Mary Anneck's house. Children and dogs were quiet and under firm control in Feather Street these days. Harold Darbyshire had gone off, grateful to be away, to a banking conference in Brussels. Even his slight relationship with Anna Mary Kinver had made him feel a marked man. He had known her, he had liked her, she had known him and apparently said she liked him. That seemed to be enough to get you

suspected. So the various writers of anonymous letters claimed. He was happy to have a rest from it all.

The police, guided by a strangely irresolute Superintendent Paul Lane, were still holding back on asking for an exhumation order on Mrs Kay Zeman. Paul
Lane had had a conference with the Chief Commander who agreed to leave it up to Lane.

Meanwhile Dr Livingstone, bright girl and prude,
if you believed Superintendent Paul Lane, had made
a decision.

She telephoned Paul Lane, her voice cool and light.
'I've come to a conclusion. You'll get my report tomorrow.'

'You don't want to dig up Ma Zeman then?'

Her voice became even cooler. 'No, but you may
want to.'

'Ah. It's poison then? So what is it?'

'It's a bit technical.'

That meant she intended to keep to the rules and he
could wait and read what she had to say. But he tried
again. As, she would discover, was his way. A nice
man, tall, fair-haired, not running to fat, but very
persistent.

'Can't you just tell me now?'

'You'll get my report in the morning. It's probably
on its way now.' Her voice was soothing and calm, like
a doctor hiding a bad report on your health from you,
but managing to give an advance warning that you
were right to be nervous at the same time.

He deserved that, she thought, as she put the receiver down. Archie Young did not deserve it, neither
did that nice John Coffin whom she had heard give a
talk at a police forum, but they would have to wait as
well.

So she went home, took a bath, put on a very nice dress from Annabelinda that had cost much more than she should have spent and went out to dinner with her boyfriend. She intended he should be a good deal more than that but she was giving him time.

She was still young enough for time to be infinitely expansive, but for other people, time was running out.

ANOTHER SCIENTIFIC REPORT was quicker at arriving on the desks of Superintendent Lane and Inspector Archie Young. In fact, they had been alerted by telephone calls at home on Friday evening. Archie Young had set up an arrangement by which the laboratory would let him know when they had the results of the tests on Tim Zeman, whatever the hour. He then passed the news on to Superintendent Paul Lane whose wife was on holiday with her mother, so that he was just thinking about taking a bottle of wine round to a certain WPC he knew.

But the message was not one that they were glad to have; it spoilt a case they thought they had tied up.

Tim Zeman had not raped Anna Mary Kinver. Whatever he had been up to on that night, he was clear on that one.

JOHN COFFIN heard the news as early as anyone, although he had set up no special contacts, maintaining a sturdy confidence in the ability of news to get to him, bad news first, good news maybe a little later. This news was neither good nor bad, but interesting.

It was Archie Young, who was taking his wife to the theatre that night and met the Chief Commander in the bar at the Theatre Workshop in the first interval, who passed it on.

'Not what we expected, is it?'

'I didn't expect anything one way or another, I was just waiting to see,' observed Coffin.

'I must admit my money was on Tim Zeman for the killing. I still think he was up to something. He's in there somewhere.' Young hated to give up on what had looked like a good idea.

The bar in the Theatre Workshop was one of the successes of Letty Bingham and her interior decorator. It had a spare, black and white charm, by Habitat out of Oggetti. When Coffin first saw it, he had thought: No one will want to linger here for a drink; it's not cosy enough. But he was wrong. People felt relaxed and cool in it, sophisticated denizens of a high tech world.

A large bronze piece of sculpture was set on a pedestal by a small fountain. It might have been a leaping fish, but it might also have been a leaping woman, except that there were no feet. But it certainly had style.

Archie Young collected his white wine. 'One of the perks of the job, having this theatre to come to, isn't it? We come regularly, Libby's dead keen. We both admire Stella Pinero, and she seems to use Lily Goldstone a lot. That's definitely another perk, she's pure gold.'

'Lily's a local,' said Coffin, picking up his own drink. He was having supper with Stella afterwards. Max from the Deli was instituting a light after-the-theatre supper service: it was an experiment, but he had great hopes of it. 'She does it for that, I think.'

The bell sounded for the next act and Archie melted into the crowd, while Coffin slowly followed. He had a front row seat, courtesy of the management, where he would have to avoid meeting Stella's eyes. Their relationship was on a knife edge at the moment. Probably they ought not to meet for a time, but when you live within a few yards of each other, this is not easy to arrange. Perhaps they weren't trying?

On the wall of the foyer through which he had to pass to get to his seat was a large poster about the charity for which the Feather Street ladies were working, a hospice for actors suffering mortal or crippling illness. A good, serious charity, they were serious ladies, the Feather Streeters. Val had done a lot for it, she would be missed.

After the performance, John Coffin waited in the basement bar for Stella to join him. They would not be the only diners, for several other tables were set out with the parties already seated. Young, bright, well-dressed people. Max was opening a bottle of champagne, and on the table rested what looked very much like a tub of caviar on ice.

Twenty, even ten, years ago such a party, such a theatre, would have been impossible to imagine in the neighbourhood. This had been working-class London, not champagne territory. Beer and jellied eels, not wine and caviar.

Nice people, he thought, sitting at his table, but making a problem for me. But as well as making his problem, he was aware they had also made his job. He wouldn't be here if the new city, with all it meant, had not been created. He himself might fail, possibly he would, but someone afterwards would succeed. The Second City was not going to die.

Stella appeared, wearing the wide black trousers so fashionable that summer, with a white silk shirt and dangling gold earrings. She waved towards the other table as she came to join him.

'Some of my keen supporters,' she said as she gave him one of her best professional kisses: a light embrace meaning nothing and transferring no lipstick. It took training to do that without blurring an outline. 'The bank they work for gave us a large donation this year. I have hopes of them sponsoring a festival next year.'

Stella was in sparkling form, which was soon explained. 'I've had a firm offer for a film, not a big part but juicy. Mostly in Spain but a bit in the States.'

'You'll take it?'

'Be a fool not to.'

'What about the theatre here?'

'It was always part of my contract with Letty that I should be allowed time away. Lily might take over. Be a great coup for the Workshop if she did, although goodness knows what sort of a repertoire she'd build up. All plays from her left-wing Marxist friends, I expect...' Stella accepted a plate of smoked salmon mousse from Max. 'No, I do Lily an injustice. She has excellent taste and a keen sense of commercial values, especially where her own money is concerned, and I think Letty will be negotiating for her to put some in.'

Letty Bingham too had a keen sense of the value of money.

'How long will you be away?'

'Oh, only a few months. Not really long...' She put her hand across the table to touch his. 'Sort us out, won't it?'

So Stella's mind had been working on the same lines as his? Stella was always shrewder than you expected.

'You mean absence making the heart grow fonder and so on?'

'Or the opposite.' Always the realist, Stella.

He caught sight of a familiar figure behind Max. 'Isn't that Fred Kinver helping out in the bar?'

Stella nodded. 'Yes, he's doing a bit of this and that.'

'How is he?'

'How do you think?'

Fred Kinver was moving around efficiently enough, but occasionally flicking a glance at the diners. The glances were cold.

'He looks as if he'd like to poison the lot of us,' said Coffin.

Stella shrugged. 'I expect he would. I think he hates everyone who is alive and not dead like his daughter.'

'Even himself?'

'Especially himself, I'd say. I'm only employing him to help his wife out. He's giving her a bad time.'

After the meal, as they crossed the courtyard to St Luke's Mansions, unwilling to end the evening, he said: 'Let's go for a walk.'

Stella looked at one delicate sandalled foot. 'Not in these shoes.'

'Put something else on, then.'

She pulled a face, but reappeared with reasonable speed wearing jeans and trainers.

'I wasn't suggesting a marathon,' he said, tucking her arm under his, 'but you've got the right idea.'

They strolled through the streets towards the river. The street lights were on, but there were still plenty of people about. Everywhere windows were wide open because of the heat, and you could see people moving about in the rooms inside, hear music and voices.

Then they were out of the noisy well-lit area into darkness. The moon had gone down.

Suddenly Stella made a protest: 'You're taking me down Rope Alley!' She moved closer to him.

'It's all right. You're with me. You're quite safe. And in case you didn't notice, a patrol car just went past and checked us... Just wanted another look around here after seeing a blow-up of one of Harry's photographs.'

Rope Alley was not empty tonight. One or two other pedestrians were filtering through it towards the main road. From the river came a ship's siren, hooting its message.

'High tide,' said Coffin. 'That's a ship going out. Sometimes I forget this is still a working river and that there are some craft on it.' A thought was taking shape in his mind.

As the other walkers came past them, he thought they looked very like sailors from one of the ships. Dutch, perhaps, or Scandinavian. A rat darted from a hole in the wall of the alley, and a cat watched it. Rope Alley was alive at night all right with its own private life.

'I don't think you forgot,' said Stella. She withdrew her arm. 'I think you brought me down here to listen.'

He laughed and took her arm again. 'Come on, let's go back.'

In companionable silence they walked back to St Luke's Mansions. When she saw the tower of St Luke's outlined against the sky, Stella said, 'I probably will take this film offer.'

'Of course you will. Silly not to.'

He kissed her gently. 'Good night, Stella, sleep well.'

From behind her door came a soft snuffle and growl. Bob was on duty.

'You know, I think I will. I don't feel quite so nervous now I've got that dog. It's a quiet night.'

He saw her safely inside, then went through his own front door and up the turret staircase. As he mounted the stairs, he thought: Someone ought to let the Zeman boy know he is off the hook. But he knew his men well enough to guess they would not do this; they would let the boy sweat a while longer to see what they could get out of him.

He looked out of the window for a moment. The night sky was calm and still, you could see the stars. As Stella had said, it was a quiet night.

Sometimes the quiet nights are the most dangerous of all.

# ELEVEN

*Saturday, June 24*

COFFIN AWOKE TO the sound of Chris Marsh's milk-float stopping in the street below. He was too far up in his turret to hear the clink of the milk bottle as it was set down, but he could imagine it. Stella Pinero had two bottles of low fat milk, but he had never discovered what she did with it, as he never saw her drink milk. He had to admit that Marsh, with all his faults, was never late on the job. If you wanted an early bottle of milk, you got it from him.

Coffin was one of the few who knew why Clare Marsh had killed herself. She had been HIV positive. Her husband knew, Coffin knew, and a few others like her doctor knew, but the boy, Jim, probably did not know. He hoped he would never have to know.

Chris Marsh sped on down to Feather Street. He liked to get his deliveries over early in the day, thus leaving him free for that life of his own that he was always going to start upon yet never seemed to achieve.

Two pints and one cream for Mrs Anneck, one pint for old Mrs Bartram next door, and three pints for the Darbyshires further along the road. He never knew what they did with the milk bottles, more went in than ever came out, he knew that much because he had to bear the cost. One New Year a whole boxful, about fifty bottles, rested on the Darbyshires' doorstep waiting for him, so they must keep them all inside the house in a big container. Every bottle was clean, though, not a sour or cruddy one in the lot. But all the Feather Street ladies were good about returning their bottles well washed. Chris gave them full marks for hygiene. Likewise for paying regularly.

Three pints of skimmed for Dr Zeman, together with some special Bulgarian yoghurt which Chris liked and ate himself so he didn't mind going to the trouble of getting it in specially for the household.

The Zemans were in trouble, as he well knew, and since he regarded himself as an expert on being in trouble, he sympathized with them. Bottle in hand, he advanced up the short garden path.

Mrs Zeman, or Dr Felicity as she was known to some people, liked her milk delivered to the front door. The ladies of Feather Street were divided on this point. Some, like Phil Darbyshire, preferred to have the bottles at the back door, near the kitchen. Others, and Mary Anneck was among them, put a container at the side of the house, where it was in the shade from the morning sun. A few issued no instructions and presumably did not care one way or another. To these he gave front door delivery since it was easier for him, less walking. Felicity Zeman had asked for the bottles to be put on the step in the porch.

To his surprise, there was a small off-white figure on the step this morning.

'Hello, Arthur,' he said. 'What are you doing here?'

Arthur was a quiet but not specially friendly dog. He stood up and stared at the milkman hopefully, but without wagging his tail.

'How did you get out?' Chris knew that Felicity Zeman was protective with the white peke, who was old and partly blind.

He saw that the door was a degree open and that Arthur had come through but had been unable to nose his way back in. This was odd, because Arthur although small and old was sturdily built.

Chris had never known the front door open before. He stood before it, holding a milk bottle, debating what to do. If anything. He could just put the bottle down, then turn and walk away.

'I ought to walk away from this. I just ought to do that.' He touched the door, gave it a tentative push.

It did not move. He gave a second shove. This time the door did move very slightly. Something was stopping it.

He tried another push, still not very hard but giving it a bit more pressure.

A hand flopped through the door at his feet.

He gave a small cry of alarm, he could feel his heart thudding faster. He swallowed hard, a little nervous lump rising in his throat.

It was a man's hand, well manicured, with fine dark hairs on the fingers.

With some relief he realized that the hand was still attached to the wrist, he could see a watch.

'Come on, Arthur.'

Taking a deep breath, he pushed the door back with some strength. Behind the door was slumped the body of Dr Leonard Zeman. He had pulled the telephone table down on the floor on top of him. It looked as though he had tried to open the door to get out and failed, sliding down against the open door.

Chris bent down. 'I don't know if you are dead or not.' He heard himself speak the words aloud. He raised his voice and called out. 'Help here, I need help.'

His voice echoed through the hall and up the stairs. No one answered. The house seemed empty.

Arthur was fussing round the body, sniffing at the face, trying to lick the hands. Chris pulled him away. The hand was still warm; Chris felt for a pulse, he thought there was a faint movement beneath his fingers. He put his hand on Dr Zeman's chest, pulling aside the pajama jacket. He must have been in bed when he became unwell.

Chris sat back on his heels. There was a heartbeat. Summoning up memories of a First-Aid course of long ago, he turned Dr Zeman on his side, then picked up the telephone. With an unsteady hand he dialled the emergency number.

Then he went to stand outside to wait for the ambulance, taking Arthur with him.

He took a long deep breath of good fresh air; he did not know what had happened in that house or where everyone was, but he knew he didn't want to stay inside.

For a moment he closed his eyes, only to open them quickly. A car had stopped behind his milk-float. He recognized it as Felicity Zeman's smart red Mercedes.

She came briskly up the path. 'What's this? What's wrong? Why are you here?' Arthur was jumping up and down, barking with excitement. 'Down Arthur.'

'It's Dr Zeman,' began Chris, 'I found him . . .'

But Felicity was already in the hall, kneeling beside her husband. She turned to Chris, who spoke before she could utter.

'I've called an ambulance. It's on its way.' He thought he could hear it now drawing up outside. In a dim kind of way, he realized his milk-float must be in the way and shouldn't he be getting on with his round?

Felicity Zeman rose to her feet. 'Where's Tim?'

Chris just shook his head speechlessly.

She ran up the stairs. Then he heard her scream.

DR ANGELA LIVINGSTONE in her thorough, unhurried way had examined the body of Val Humberstone for the cause of death. She had found normal coronary arteries and no obvious post-mortem signs to give her an indication of what that cause was. She was too experienced and too canny to find this unusual. People did drop dead and yet still appear to have normal coronary arteries. Death was unfair and unpredictable sometimes.

She moved on to do a screening of the blood and other body fluids for a number of substances. Some traces she found there made her thoughtful.

It had been at this point she had asked for a PM on Mrs Zeman. You could call it just curiosity.

Then she had done a muscle biopsy, because what she was looking for was stored in the muscle as well as in the blood serum. There are, of course, changes in the blood serum after death, but she had what she wanted.

Finally and triumphantly, she did a monoclonal antibody test.

Then she knew how Val Humberstone had died.

So she duly put together her report, despatched it through the usual channels so that it would be on certain desks in the morning. Then she went out to dinner in good spirits.

Over dinner, she said blithely. 'I've just finished an interesting PM.'

'Oh yes?' Her boyfriend was a doctor too, so he could take in the notion of an interesting PM over his dinner without ceasing in his consumption of grilled steak and salad. 'More wine?' He had cooked the steak himself, allowing Angela to mix the salad.

Angela accepted the wine and rested her elbows on the table. They were eating in his kitchen. She was prepared to be confidential to Dr Mark Allen while maintaining a reserve towards her police bosses. They must learn how to treat a professional.

'Death was due to overdose of glycoside. Massive dose.'

Mark looked interested. 'Accident? Wrong prescription?'

'Don't know. That's for the police to find out . . . I think it might be murder.'

Now Mark did stop eating, halted in mid-bite by his surprise. 'Good lord, that's an unusual poison for homicide, isn't it?'

'Unique, I should think.'

'Got any reason for thinking it's murder?'

Angela nodded. She had some reason. An oddness she had noticed, but she was too discreet to pass this strange fact on to Mark in what might be a tricky case, and one in which she would almost certainly be a witness for the prosecution. 'I don't see it as an accident,' she said.

Her conscience was clear. She had done a good job, had played a sort of game with people she did not much like, but no harm could come of that, because tomorrow the report would be on the desks of the investigators, one copy each. She had kept the rules.

JOHN COFFIN also slept with a clear conscience. He had been too long at the game to harrow himself unnecessarily. After being disturbed by Chris Marsh on his milk-float, he had gone back to sleep, falling into one of those nightmares he had experienced lately which centred around Stella. She was always off-stage in these dreams, he never saw her, but she was just round the corner and in terrible danger. She had screamed, he never heard the scream, it was always as if it had just died away, leaving only the echo in his ears. He always awoke at this point, surfacing with the relieved feeling that it was a dream after all.

One day he might tell Stella, but not just yet.

The telephone rang somewhere in his flat, he had to remember where he had deposited it last. Stirring himself and clearing the fog of sleep from his brain, he remembered carrying it upstairs last night.

Must be in the room somewhere. He stared around. The sound was very close. Underneath him, he was sleeping on it. He reached under the pillow to answer it.

Because his mind was full of Stella, it was the greater shock when it was her voice heard on the telephone.

It was vibrant with alarm, she was sounding a kind of tocsin, with those famous deep tones thrilling the sound waves.

'John, I thought you ought to know, perhaps you do know, I think something terrible has happened at the Zemans... Jim Marsh came in to collect Bob, I've got an early call for a TV session, and he says he saw ambulances outside their house. Do you know what it is?'

'No, I don't know anything.' But someone had better tell me.

He hoisted himself out of bed, still carrying the telephone. 'I'll let you know, Stella. If I can, can't promise.' Events sometimes ran too fast to pass on news.

'Jim said it looked pretty bad.' After a very short pause, she said, 'He thinks he saw Fred Kinver down there. I thought I ought to tell you. It doesn't seem a good idea for him to be there, whatever is going on.'

'I'll let you know what I find out. You get off now, Stella.'

'I ought. I think the taxi's there now. I'm playing ten years younger and that does take some making up to.'

'You go, Stella.'

Neither of them knew that the Paper Man had made his move.

The telephone rang again almost at once. The caller was Archie Young, never averse to a chance to talk to the Guv'nor. He was sharp enough to know it could do him no harm at all.

'Thought I should report, sir. I'm at Dr Zeman's house in Feather Street. The Zeman boy is dead. Don't know the cause yet. Or whether it's suicide. Could be. If so, he tried to take his father with him.'

'Is Dr Zeman . . . ?'

'No.' Archie Young got it out quickly. 'He's not dead. Nearly, but not quite. Poison. We don't know what yet, of course. The police surgeon has had a look but hasn't said much.' Didn't know what to say, was Young's opinion, but in any case police surgeons were a cautious lot, not given to committing themselves to premature judgements. Especially this one; Dr Wright had arrived to pronounce Timmy Zeman dead, and he never said one word, if silence would do.

'I'll be down.'

'Right, sir, be expecting you. The Superintendent's on his way,' said Young dutifully, returning to the chaos inside the Feather Street house.

He had not been the first police arrival at the Zeman household. The very first had been two uniformed men in a police car. They had been followed at speed by a CID detective-sergeant.

He himself had got there as the police sergeant had finished his examination. Dr Leonard Zeman had been taken to hospital. Felicity was still in the house, and Chris Marsh, his milk round unfinished, was sitting slumped on a chair in the hall. He looked thoroughly miserable.

But he was willing enough to tell what he knew.

'I was walking up the path with the milk bottle when I saw Arthur, he's the dog.' Arthur was also present, sitting under the chair, eyes alert. Every so often he growled at the passing police feet. It was only a matter of time until he bit someone. 'I wondered what he was doing there. Then I saw the door was slightly open, he must have got out. I wondered why he didn't go back.'

'So you went up to the door?' asked Young.

'Yes, but I've already said all this to the sergeant.'

'I want to hear too.'

Chris started again. 'I went to the door and pushed it. Thought I'd let the dog in. He's never allowed out on his own. But the door wouldn't move. Or not much. I realized something was stopping it.'

From underneath the chair Arthur gave a low, soft growl. He had made his decision, he did not like this particular policeman, didn't care for his voice. He was the one to go for.

'Go on,' said Young, thinking that if you had to have a dog, why not have a proper one?

'So I pushed the door again and then I saw a hand. It was Dr Zeman. He was lying there on the floor, pressed against the door.'

'Could you describe what you saw?'

'He'd pulled the table where there was a telephone over and had the telephone down on top of him. I reckon he'd been trying to telephone for help, then felt he needed air, but collapsed.'

Seemed a rational explanation, thought Young, but it was not for Chris Marsh to say what was what. So he nodded. 'And then?'

'I thought he was dead, but I felt his pulse and there seemed to be one. That was when I called for an ambulance. Then Dr Felicity came in.'

'What did she do?'

'She looked after her husband. Then she said where was her son. I didn't know. I had shouted for him, but he hadn't appeared. She ran up the stairs and I heard her scream.'

Chris Marsh had told his story so far with some vividness. He went on: 'I went up the stairs after her when she screamed.'

He paused.

'Do you want to stop?'

'No, I'll go on. Timmy Zeman was on the bed, half on it, half off. I could see by his face that he was gone. Eyes closed, but he looked dead.'

'What did you do then?'

'I didn't do anything else. I'd already called an ambulance, but Dr Felicity did some more telephoning.

To the hospital, I think. Then ambulances and the police started arriving. Dr Felicity said—'

'I'll talk to Dr Zeman myself.'

Felicity Zeman had, with difficulty, been prevented from going with her husband, and was now sitting in the dining-room waiting to be questioned.

Chris considered. 'Is this a statement?'

'No, just questions to put me in the picture.'

'Ah. Right. Can I go, then? I'd like to get on with my milk round. My customers will be wondering where I am.'

'They'll have to wait a bit longer, I'm afraid.'

'Can I have a drink of water? A cup of tea would be better.'

At that moment the police surgeon came through the hall with his bag, and John Coffin arrived at the front door, together with a police photographer.

They had been watched by a small cluster of neighbours, several dogs of the district, one in charge of Jim Marsh, others running free, and a hidden company of cats.

'Wouldn't advise you to eat or drink anything in this house,' said the police surgeon as he swept through. 'Wouldn't advise it at all.'

Arthur leapt from beneath the chair and fastened his teeth in Young's ankle. It was hard, covered in something rough, but just chewy enough to give job satisfaction. Archie Young swore.

JOHN COFFIN toured the scene of the crime quietly, not saying much. He had talked to Superintendent Paul Lane in the police car parked at the kerb, so he knew the details, such as they were.

'Has Mrs Zeman explained why she wasn't in the house when her husband and son were taken ill?'

'She was on call at the hospital and had been out all night, dealing with a series of emergencies. That appears to be true.'

Coffin nodded. 'Has she said anything of interest?'

'Not said much at all. She's in a state of some distress but not talking a lot. Takes everyone differently, some talk their heads off, she's just gone quiet.'

'Is the cause of death known yet?'

'No, we ought to know more during the day. The hospital might have something to say about what has made Leonard Zeman ill, and killed Tim. Not natural death, though. The third death in that family in as many weeks.'

'Yes, I haven't overlooked Val Humberstone. Well, we ought to know about her soon. Do you think Tim Zeman's death is suicide?'

'Could be. Or some sort of accident. But he had something on his mind, even if he wasn't the one who raped Anna Mary Kinver. It's an explanation to think he killed himself. He may not have meant to harm his father.'

'Leonard Zeman may have something to say when he comes round.'

'If he comes round... Funny, the wife not being there. I know she was on call and all that.'

'You think she tried to kill them both?'

'It bears thinking about. She might not have intended to kill them, just punish them a bit. Poisoning is a funny business and often a family affair. You know that as well as I do. I'm thinking hard about her, I can tell you.'

He added: 'By the way, the man on the front door says he saw Fred Kinver hanging around. Knows him by sight. He must have got wind of trouble here. Like a vulture. Can't blame him really, I suppose.'

'Is he still there?'

'The constable spoke to him and he went off. I've had reports that he's been seen hanging around Feather Street on and off lately. There have been complaints. He doesn't do anything apparently, just looks. Half crazed with grief, I suppose. I accept that but it won't do. We'll have to have a quiet word.'

ON HIS OWN, Coffin went over the house from top to bottom. He saw at once that it was one of the nicest in Feather Street. It had been modernized in a discreet way without ruining the character of the Victorian house. Walls had not been knocked down, rooms had not been thrown together to produce long tunnels with windows at each end as had happened with the Annecks, nor great extensions tacked on at the end as Harold Darbyshire had so unwisely commissioned and now regretted because his rates were higher and his home filled with the children of his friends who brought nothing but trouble with them. Drugs, shop-lifting and murder haunted his respectable sleep. No, the Zeman house had new wiring and new plumbing, but the kitchen was still in the basement just as the original builder had placed it.

Coffin started there, saw the remains of a meal tidily stacked away ready to go in the dishwasher, and concluded that the family had eaten but had not got around to doing the washing-up. Perhaps they never did do so at night, or perhaps the two male Zemans had felt too ill. Dr Felicity, of course, had been called out to the hospital.

Had she eaten? Something to find out.

He walked up the stairs, enjoying the soft brown carpet and polished mahogany banisters on the stairs. The ground floor had been old Dr Zeman's consulting rooms and had been left as they were by Leonard Zeman, who still saw a few private patients there. He had obviously been working in this room the night before because of the spread of papers on the old-fashioned roll-top desk. A chair was turned over, possibly he had already begun to feel ill, but otherwise the room was orderly.

In a smaller room across the way Dr Felicity was sitting in an armchair staring straight in front of her with dry eyes. Arthur was resting at her feet. Coffin left them both there.

Upstairs was a large room which still deserved the name drawing-room with soft pale furnishings, pictures on the walls and bowls of flowers everywhere.

On the next floor were bedrooms and bathrooms. In the big front room the bed was untouched, no one had slept here. Dr Zeman had got ready for bed, but had never got there. That gave a time indication of a sort.

In a back room the body of Timmy Zeman still lay.

He had been examined by the police surgeon, photographed and in a few minutes now would be removed to the policy mortuary, where Anna Mary Kinver still rested, but for the moment he and Coffin were alone together.

He had been tidied up, and there were signs that he had vomited, but that apart, Timmy looked as if he had died in deep and peaceful sleep. It could be suicide, Coffin thought, but if so, why did Dad join in? Or was he dragged or fell?

Suicide, double suicide attempt, or accident, or murder? You could take your pick.

The bedroom was orderly enough, a boy's room, with posters on the walls and magazines and books piled high on a table. There was a record-player, a transistor and TV set with a video recorder. Timmy Zeman lived up here, it was the centre of his life. Here, if anywhere, the mystery might be solved.

Coffin looked at the magazines. They were what you might expect of a boy with a range of interests. *Radio* and *TV Times*, current issues. The *Scientific American*, *True Crimes*, *History Today*, *Private Eye*.

He read a lot. A row of poetry books: the *Oxford Book of English Verse*, Tennyson, Browning, Swinburne, and then more modern poets like Larkin and Hughes and Jennings.

At the bottom of the pile were two magazines called *Apart*. Coffin had met this monthly before. It was quite respectable, but not on general sale, it was put out by a private club. These two magazines had something to tell him about the lad.

He felt he had walked a little way with Timmy Zeman. 'I too have lived in Arcadia,' he thought. Tim had been looking for Arcadia, for poetry and love and happiness, but maybe in the wrong place. Probably a nice boy, after all. But even nice boys did terrible things.

Coffin went downstairs to the room where Felicity Zeman was sitting. She stood up as soon as she saw him. 'I know you. You came to the opening of the new wing at the hospital. But you were in uniform.'

'I do have a rather grand affair I wear on some public occasions. That was one of them.'

'I want to go and see my husband,' she said. 'Timmy's dead. I can't help him. I might be able to help Leonard.'

'Can I have a few words with you now? I won't press you, but it would help.'

At first Felicity did not move, then she slowly retreated back to the chair. 'Please sit down. This is still my house and I am still the hostess, I can still ask that.'

'You mustn't feel under threat, Mrs Zeman.'

'Oh, but I do. My son is dead, my husband might be soon. That other policeman let me know I was under suspicion.'

'I'm sure he did not mean to do that,' said Coffin, deciding to have a word with Paul Lane.

'Oh, but he did. He suspects me. So do you, probably. It's your job to do so.'

'We don't know yet that a crime has been committed.'

'One has,' said Felicity Zeman with conviction. 'I know it and you know it. Don't let's play games.'

There was a pause while the two parties regrouped. Then Coffin started again.

'You were called out on duty last night, so I believe?'

'Yes. In the middle of dinner. One crisis led to another. I stayed all night.'

'That couldn't have been predicted?'

She shrugged. 'Not by me. But how can I prove that?'

'My question wasn't meant aggressively. So you didn't eat the meal? What was it?'

'Gazpacho soup. It was a hot night. Then chocolate pudding.'

'Who cooked it?'

'I did. If you can call it cooking. The soup you really just make from raw vegetables with bread and throw in ice-cubes at the last minute. The chocolate pudding was made weeks ago. I took it out of the freezer.'

'Who made the pudding?'

'I think Val did. It was her recipe.'

'And you ate nothing of the meal?'

'A mouthful of the soup, that was all I had time for.'

'It tasted all right?'

She shrugged. 'A bit crunchy, but then it always does.'

'And you suffered no ill-effects?'

'As you see, I am perfectly well. I quite see that very nearly proves my guilt...'

'Please, Mrs Zeman.'

'I am a doctor too,' she said coldly. 'And I expect you will say I killed Val as well. She was my husband's mistress, as I imagine you know or will discover. That gives me a motive.'

'Does it?' he said gravely. 'Did you think it did?'

'There are some people who might think divorce better than killing someone, I might be one.'

'But possession comes into it, doesn't it, Dr Zeman?'

'So you do think I poisoned them. Do you think I would poison my son?'

'No, not on purpose.'

'And not by accident.'

'No, I give you that.'

'Thanks,' she said tartly, too exhausted to be angry.

They sat for a moment in silence. Then Coffin said: 'Before Val Humberstone died she asked to see me. She said she had something to tell me about Timmy. I got the impression she believed it would clear him of suspicion of killing Anna Mary Kinver.'

'In that case I would have a very good motive for keeping her alive, I assure you. At least long enough for her to tell you whatever it was. I loved my son.'

'I know,' said Coffin.

She stood up and went to the window, a tall, graceful figure, managing to retain a certain style even amid grief and tension after a night without sleep.

'I think I know what Val would have told you about Tim. He wouldn't have been grateful. Tim was not in love with Anna Mary. He may have experimented with sex with her, but it was because he was trying to work out his own sexuality.' She shook her head. 'He didn't really go for girls. If he was in love with anyone it was not Anna Mary but a boy he met at a disco.' She turned back to face him, and he saw tears in her eyes. 'Poor girl, poor boy.'

'You can go and see your husband if you wish, Dr Zeman.'

'Thank you. I suppose there will be a policeman on guard?'

'Yes. Don't let that worry you.'

'Anna Mary, Val and Timmy, it's all one case, isn't it?'

'I believe so,' said Coffin. 'All one case.'

She picked up Arthur and watched him go, stroking the dog and holding him close. Looking back at her, Coffin thought she was weeping freely. Just as well, he thought, she deserves a relief. He had to admit to a certain admiration for Dr Felicity Zeman. She was beautiful and clever.

He admitted to a weakness for beautiful and clever ladies.

AS HE WALKED THROUGH the hall, Coffin saw Archie Young. 'How's the ankle?'

Archie Young scowled. 'Not too bad, but I'm going to get a tetanus injection.'

'Don't forget rabies as well,' said Coffin as he passed through the front door.

He made for his car. Although it was still early morning, Feather Street was awake and taking observation. The curtains at the house next door only half hid the woman gazing out. Further down the road a man was cleaning his windows while staring at the Zeman house.

Across the road, a figure was hunched: Fred Kinver.

Coffin went across. 'I think you should go home, Fred.'

'Want to see what's going on.'

'Go home, or I'll have someone take you home.'

'They're dead, aren't they? Good. I'm glad. It's what I wanted. You won't get me for wanting that. I know you, I've gone into your career. Made it my business. Making a book on you. I know what you've done, what you can do and what you can't do. And you're just. Hard but just. They all say that. And justice for my girl was all I ever wanted. If you can't get it, make it, that's what I say.'

He's mad, thought Coffin, temporarily perhaps, but for the moment quite crazed. King Lear must have looked like that.

'Someone will drive you home,' he said to Fred Kinver. 'I think your wife must be worrying. And stay there, until I tell you to come out.'

For his own safety, for everyone's safety, in the present emotional state of the area, he was better tethered.

That day, as on several days previously, without realizing it John Coffin had set eyes on the Paper Man.

# TWELVE

*Sunday, June 25*

ONE OF THE disadvantages of his position, contrary to what might have been expected, was that John Coffin was not always the first to know the news.

When Dr Angela Livingstone heard of the events in Feather Street, she felt alarmed, and even guilty. Was it her fault in any way? No, not so, surely not. She would like to have spoken to the Chief Commander John Coffin himself, as her spies told her that he was a nice man and eminently approachable. But protocol forbade it, the system had to be honoured even by one anxious to purge her soul. Even to a rebel who liked to stamp on the rules.

So she put aside any remaining hostility (and after all, the man had only made a pass at her, didn't all policemen do it, one way or another?) and telephoned Superintendent Paul Lane at once.

His line was busy so she made a face at the telephone and got through to the hospital to find out how Leonard Zeman was.

'Holding his own,' she was told; she was well aware that this vague phrase might mean anything. You could be terminally ill and the ward sister would say this soothing nonsense.

But she knew one of the registrars there. 'Can I speak to Dr Erskine? Say it's Dr Angela Livingstone.'

'Bleeping Dr Erskine,' said the telephonist cheerfully. 'He won't be pleased, he was just going for a cup of coffee.'

Tough, thought Angela, and hung on. Very soon a sleepy voice said it had been up all night and what did Angela want?

'Are you looking after Leonard Zeman?'

'Not directly. Been observing the case.' Leonard was a case, no longer a person. He would only become a person again if he recovered and left hospital, and not a fellow medical practitioner till he took up work again.

'How is he? Really how is he?'

'He is in a small side ward, with a policeman outside the door, and he is deeply comatose, but his blood pressure is rising. He may come out of it or he may not, your guess is as good as mine. Friend of yours?'

'Only know him by name. What's the diagnosis?'

'Angel dear, did you drag me away from my coffee just to ask that?'

'From the sound of it, you brought the coffee with you and are still drinking it.'

'Up all night, dear. As to the diagnosis, you know my boss. Still sitting on the fence.'

'Tell him to think about one of the glycosides.'

'Good lord,' said Perry Erskine. 'You don't say. I'll pass it along. Get a Brownie point.'

'Don't quote me. But I feel guilty.'

'Why! You didn't give him an overdose, did you? Must have been a massive one, by the way.'

'No, I didn't, of course not, you fool.'

But maybe, she thought, as she put down the telephone, which was making noises about Why not dinner together, Angel, if I had been quicker in passing on the information about Val Humberstone, this need not have happened.

She was still young enough to think that somehow she could alter the course of events.

When she spoke to Superintendent Lane she was blunt: 'If you have read my report on Val Humberstone, and I don't know if you've had time yet, you will see I say she died from taking too much of one of the glycoside drugs.'

'I have read the report, it's on my desk now. Tell me what these glycosides are?'

'They are given as a treatment for diseases of the cardiovascular system.'

'Heart trouble, in other words?'

'That's right. In the quantity that I reckon the dead woman took them, they would produce heart failure, though.'

'Just like that?'

'No, probably not. She'd feel sleepy, begin to be unwell, the heart would become violently irregular, she would fall asleep and never wake up.'

'I see. Not a common poison, is it?'

'I don't know if it's ever been used before. You'd know more about that, perhaps. We might consult the Forensic Science people at Harrogate. They may know of other cases.'

'I think I know of two others now,' said Paul Lane. 'You'd better have a look at Tim Zeman, and I think you'd better have a look at Mrs Kay Zeman. I'll get an exhumation order.'

Without satisfaction, he contemplated the fact that he had a case of mass murder on his hands, a multiple poisoning, the wiping out of an entire family.

Paul Lane was an ambitious man who was keeping an anxious eye on the shape of his career: he had done well, but he wanted to do better. A badly run case at this stage in his professional life could spoil every-thing. There were a lot of ways you could fall off the ladder in the police and he knew most of them. Had fallen off a rung himself in the past, then climbed back on again, had seen colleagues fall off and never get back. He did not want to be one of them.

He was only too aware that a bright and hungry generation was coming up behind him. Women too. In his heart he hated the idea of women in the police, but it didn't do to say so. He liked women, in many ways he liked them very much, but he did not want to com-pete with a woman.

There were nasty aspects to this case that he was as aware of as John Coffin. The media were already paying a lot of attention to the murder of Anna Mary Kinver. Every day there was a paragraph or a TV in-terview about it. There was tension bubbling away just below the surface in Leathergate and Spinnergate. Any day now, for any cause, it could spill over. A multiple poison case involving a family already named in the Kinver murder, already the subject of hostile specu-lation, might just do it.

Rationally, it shouldn't, because the Zemans now looked more like victims, but reason did not come into civil disturbance.

One Zeman, however, remained totally unharmed.

'These tablets,' he said. 'Only a doctor could pre-scribe them?'

'Yes,' said Angela Livingstone. She was still keep-ing to herself one vital piece of information of which she had not seen the significance. 'Yes, I'm afraid so.'

'I hate to think of a doctor doing a poisoning. Old-fashioned of me, but there it is. Of course, we know they do it.'

'Not many of them.'

'We don't get to know about the successful ones,' said Lane gloomily. 'However, patients can save up tablets, I suppose, and use them. Suicides do it, so murderers could. Right, so we shall have to start looking among our suspects for someone with heart trouble who is taking . . . what did you call it?'

'Glycosides. Trade name: Digoxin.'

Paul Lane felt they were almost on speaking terms as he put the receiver down. How would it be if he asked her for a drink? Ring up with some query about drugs, and heaven knows he would probably have one, consult her, and take it from there. She was a nice woman, and there might be, really, if one was lucky, a special relationship.

Meanwhile, a case conference was called for that morning, Sunday though it was, in which he would be requesting that all the local doctors (with special reference to both the Zeman doctors) be asked about patients on Digoxin. He must practise saying the name.

He wrote on a pad in front of him: Digoxin.

In his experience, doctors were not inclined to be helpful about their patients. The Zeman record of prescriptions would have to be opened to him. He thought he could force that opening.

And doctors only handed out prescriptions, very few these days ran their own pharmacy. So there would be all the local chemists to question.

He had been one of the foot soldiers himself once, so had Archie Young and so had the top man himself, they all knew what that meant in the way of trudging around and asking questions and getting no answers or not the ones you wanted. But it had to be done.

As with the conference of all those concerned. This was now a Major Incident with everything it entailed in the way of Receivers, Indexers, Statement Readers and Action Allocators. He hoped the computers did not go down. All the computers, nationwide, Force to Force, were supposed to be able to speak to each other, but in his experience this did not always happen. He relied on the computers, you had to, a great tool, but when they failed you, it was as if you had ropes hobbling your feet.

In his time he had enjoyed the setting up of a MIRIAM room, now he was the overseer, a boss figure, and the mundane task of creating the room fell to the likes of Archie Young.

He called his wife and told her that he would be late back, not to expect him, he was sorry to miss Sunday lunch but she knew what was going on.

She did know. Mrs Lane always knew a bit more than he thought she did, she was an experienced police wife, an old hand at the game, she knew about the drinking parties, the odd woman, but she knew also about the grind, the strain, and the long hours of work. Provided he kept it under control, she adapted herself to it. She also had what she called her 'little hobbies' and one day, when it suited her, she would let him know about them. It made for give and take.

She loved her husband, but she feared for him in the violence that surrounded him in his work. It was a turbulent world he faced where the police were as often as not the victims. They had moved into Spinnergate when the new job came up, and although she enjoyed her sparkling bright flat with its views of the

river, she sometimes felt nervous of the district outside. The children were grown up and away from
home, she was on her own a lot. New riches and the
memory of old poverties don't make easy friends. The
natives were definitely unfriendly.

So she washed her hair and took herself out. She
had in any case not cooked Sunday lunch, gambling
on Paul not being home.

BY LATE AFTERNOON Dr Leonard Zeman was conscious and able to talk. Archie Young went down to
see him in his hospital room. A nurse stayed with him
and a youthful doctor, called Erskine, hovered. Rather
more closely than Inspector Young, who had a sergeant with him, thought necessary.

To the first question, Leonard Zeman said that he
couldn't seem to remember much, except beginning to
feel ill, trying to telephone as well as wanting air.

Had he opened the front door?

Yes, he thought he might have done. Yes, he was
sure he had. The dog was there with him, he remembered the dog.

'The dog was seen on the doorstep, he couldn't get
back in. The milkman saw him and then found you.
You probably owe it to the milkman that you are
alive.' A few hours more, the medical opinion had
suggested, and recovery would have been unlikely.

'You had a meal, Dr Zeman? You remember eating?'

'Yes, I had supper with Tim.' He had been told
about his son, but Archie Young doubted if he had
taken it in.

'Do you remember what you had?'

Leonard Zeman seemed to dig into his memory. 'We had cold soup, gazpacho. I remember the ice. Then a chocolate pudding. Then raspberries and cream. I think that was it.'

He lay back on his pillows. 'I gather I was poisoned. From the questions you ask, you must think it was in the food.'

'Just trying to establish just how you got it, Doctor.'

'There won't be any of the soup left. I poured it away. Might be some of the pudding. I don't remember about it.'

'There wasn't.'

'Timmy finished it up, I suppose.'

And got far more of the poison than you did, and hence died? Young thought. From the way Leonard Zeman spoke, Young guessed he had understood about his son.

'I'd like to know what poison I've ingested. I'm trying to work out what it could have been.'

'I wouldn't bother with it, Dr Zeman.'

Leonard Zeman closed his eyes. He said: 'Where's my wife? Has she gone home? She was here, I know.'

The nurse spoke before Young could open his mouth. 'All the time, Dr Zeman. When she saw you were going to be all right, we persuaded her to go home for some rest. You're out of the wood now, you know.'

'I ought to be with her.'

He had understood about his son, Young thought, and his mind was working on the problem with more sharpness with every minute that passed. He wasn't in a happy position when it could be that either his wife or his son, who might have been a suicidal murderer, had poisoned him.

Young stayed for a while longer, asking a range of questions about the family and their habits, more to assess how they went on than from any hope of positive evidence one way or another. But the nurse started to make murmuring noises about tiring Dr Zeman, so he got up and left.

Leonard Zeman held out his hand and hung on to Young's for a bit. 'If I think of anything I'll tell you.'

'Thank you, sir. Anything. Be glad of it.'

When Inspector Young and his sergeant got outside, he found that someone had kicked the side of his car, damaging the paintwork.

Outside a hospital, he thought, and on a Sunday too.

As he drove back to his office, he saw a spiral of smoke in the distance. Fire-engines were already rushing that way.

Down by the river, he thought, or was it? As he drove the acrid smell of burning came up his nose. Perhaps nearer than the docks? He couldn't be sure.

Definitely not a nice Sunday.

# THIRTEEN

*Still on that same Sunday*

SUNDAY WAS A DAY for burning.

But not down by the docks, Archie Young found out as he drove towards his office, much nearer home.

Some sod, as his sergeant delicately put it, had driven an old banger into the car park of the new police station, where security was not what it should be, and then set light to it. Blazing merrily, it had then exploded and looked as though it might set light to several other cars, including the sergeant's own. The fire brigade had then arrived in force and blanketed every vehicle in sight in foam. One of those covered was Superintendent Paul Lane's own special Rover, and another belonged to the Chief Commander. There were many others, and since everyone feared that the foam could be damaging to paintwork, chrome and internal upholstery, their owners were not happy men.

Since the whole building had been evacuated on the fire chief's orders in case there was an explosion, all concerned had a full view of the spectacle.

That was the best and biggest fire, but there were also smaller fires in two empty houses just finished and awaiting occupation, and another fire in the site manager's office on a new flat and marina complex just started. A guard dog had been drugged.

A fire that never took place was in the courtyard of St Luke's Mansions between the Theatre Workshop

and the old church itself, now awaiting its new life as
the main theatre. In this courtyard a small bonfire had
been built, but no attempt had been made to light it.
Stella Pinero interpreted it as a threat.

She surveyed it late that afternoon in company with
Lily Goldstone.

'It's a warning.'

'Nothing personal,' said Lily easily. She had a riv-
erside flat, she had been born locally, some of her
family still lived here, she felt she spoke for the whole
neighbourhood.

'I think it is. Someone doesn't like me.'

'The fire never happened.'

'I'm to wait for it. Next it will happen. Or something worse.'

'Don't think bad thoughts.' Lily was very nearly on
the point of giving up Marx and taking up the Master
of the Karma, a local seer, who had beautiful eyes and
lovely hands. At the moment, she was riding both
horses at once, a feat only Lily Goldstone could
achieve. 'You bring on yourself the fate you fear.'

'Thanks, Lily.'

Together, they cleared away the bonfire materials,
old boxes, newspapers and rubbish. It looked as
though several dustbins had been emptied in their
courtyard. It was all rather smelly and Stella wrinkled
her nose distastefully. She had a nasty feeling she recognized some of her own rubbish.

Stella had returned from her filming the day before
to hear the news about Tim Zeman. By the time she
got back, it was known that Dr Zeman would survive. John Coffin had come down to tell her himself,
they had a quiet drink in her flat and he told her not
to worry.

As is so often the case with reassurance, she felt more worried afterwards, although she tried to hide it. Bob knew this fact, and leaned heavily on her feet, staring at her with loving eyes. She was his now, and he was hers.

The Sunday of the fires worried them both. They crept out together to look at some of the conflagrations, Stella telling Bob that they ought to know what was going on even if it frightened them.

A crowd had gathered to watch the scene at the police station, at the heart of it a silent, watchful group of youths. After a bit, they melted away and reassembled outside the Zeman house. By now other onlookers had gone and only a uniformed constable remained outside the front door. He eyed the youths warily but did nothing, except radio in a report. Then a tall, scrawny lad kicked the side of Felicity Zeman's car, and another threw a stone through the rear window. Then they ran.

Another small gang was touring the area near the fire on the new estate. Hanging about, doing nothing much, but very clearly in evidence.

For a short while they coalesced with the first group, then they split up into several small parties, and roamed the district. Prowl cars kept up a quiet watch, and an All Points Bulletin sent out the message that there might be trouble on the way, and to watch for gatherings of youths.

By evening on that Sunday, they had all disappeared. Plotting something worse, was the police judgement.

At some point, a joker was able to paint on the garage wall behind the Zeman's Feather Street house, the message: GLAD THERE GONE.

Silently a group of Feather Street ladies, headed by Phil Darbyshire and Mary Anneck, scrubbed it out. They did not comment on the spelling but it added to the fury with which they worked. They were assisted by their children, unwilling conscripts.

Phil said to her son and daughter: 'If I ever catch either of you two doing anything like that or mixing with those who do, I will kill you personally. That's a promise.'

'We wouldn't,' they said, speaking as one.

'And the form that killing will take will be the cutting off of all financial support, other than plain food and a bed for the night. It will be death by monetary starvation and you will find that very painful. And you can take that seriously.'

They had been taking things seriously for some time.

The emptying of the streets was noted by the police.

'Retiring and regrouping to think up something else, the louts,' said Paul Lane sourly.

He and Archie Young were having a private conference with the Chief Commander in his office. Coffin had made it clear that he had a personal interest in all this business.

Lane had had no lunch and was very hungry. Archie had sped home to a meal cooked by his wife, and had since eaten some scrambled eggs in the canteen. He felt he could go on all night.

'I know one or two of the faces that I've seen hanging around. Could have been involved in the car window smash, their style.' Archie Young had been offered and was not drinking a cup of tea; he would have preferred beer or whisky, but this had not been on show and from the ironic look in the Old Man's eyes was not going to be. Tales said that he had been a bit of a lad himself in his day, but he was so respectable now it was painful. 'All this disturbance, fires, bricks, the lot, is linked up with the Kinver case and the Zeman deaths somehow. They're exploiting the situation, but there's real feeling there. You agree, don't you, sir? I don't suppose one of them killed the Zeman boy?' He sounded wistful. 'I wouldn't mind getting Terry Graham for it, if I could. I hate his guts. Or Ron Slater, he's worse. All that Planter Estate gang are bad.'

'I don't think they could lay hands on the Digoxin, or knew what it was if they did,' said Coffin absently. 'Or find the means of getting it into the food.'

'I might take one or two of them in and see what I can get out of them. They might have robbed a chemist's shop. Boots in Paradise Street was broken into last week.'

'Still got to find the means of administration.'

'If I thought they had the drug, I wouldn't worry about anything else.' He thought about what he had just said, and decided it wasn't such a clever thing to have voiced. He was glad to be in the company of two senior officers, drinking with them, even if only tea, but it was a burden to him too. 'What I mean is, if they had the drug, we would be more than half way there. We know the motive: one, they're wiping out the family they think responsible for the Kinver kid; two, it's a class thing. Never mind that the Zemans have lived here forever, it's a Them and Us thing.'

'There's something in that,' admitted Paul Lane. 'Get Graham and Slater in. Question them. It's a start.'

'You don't know yet in which food the poison was hidden,' said Coffin, still pursuing his own silent train of thought.

'Dr Livingstone thinks the soup is the most likely. It would hide the flavour and the rough texture of the soup would hide the slight grittiness. She also thinks a higher concentration of poison per mouthful could be achieved in the soup as opposed to the chocolate pudding. If the pudding had been in individual helpings that would have been different, but apparently it wasn't.'

'And there is none left?'

'No, it was all eaten but the dishes were left unwashed. A forensic team is going over the kitchen to see what it can find.'

'The pudding came from the freezer?'

Young consulted his notes. 'Yes, Mrs Zeman took it out. But she says she did not make it, the pudding was made by Val Humberstone. It seems chocolate cakes, puddings and biscuits were her speciality.'

Coffin realized he was about to make himself unpopular with his colleagues. Interference, would they call it?

'I had a look round the Feather Street house where Val Humberstone died. Of course, you will have done so too.' Silence from both men. Inspector Young had had a look, Paul Lane had not, he had other things to do that day but he was not going to say so. Young was well aware that Coffin was going to claim to have seen something that no one else had done. He sighed.

Lane said, half defensively: 'It was before we had really tied Miss Humberstone's death in with anything.' He himself had been convinced it was a natural death, and had not welcomed any other suggestion.

Life was difficult enough as it was. But he had had to agree that an autopsy was a good idea, he had protected himself. In a longish police career, he had learnt how to do that with some success.

He had also learned how to listen to a superior; he listened now.

'We agree that the dog, Bob, was poisoned too? When I had a look round the bedroom in the Zeman house that day, I saw a plate with a few crumbs but a licked look. I think it had had cakes or biscuits on it that the dog finished up. Miss Humberstone had eaten most, probably, so she got most of the drug. She died, Bob recovered.'

'I remember the plate,' admitted Young. 'I think the biscuits must have been chocolate biscuits.'

'So do we think that chocolate pudding held the poison in the second poisoning?' asked Lane.

'Possibly.'

'I'll get the forensic team on to it. They may get traces out of the freezer or the dishwasher.'

'Two deaths from poisoned chocolate. Well, it has a strong flavour and I understand biscuit crumbs and brandy were part of the recipe,' said Lane. 'Homemade, too. I'm not sure I will want to eat home-baked chocolate cake again.'

'Oh, if your wife cooks it . . .' Young spoke happily. He trusted his wife.

'Yes, my wife,' agreed Lane uneasily, resolving to pay her more attention in future. Not that she seemed to do much cooking these days. What did she do with her time when he wasn't there?

'More than two deaths, perhaps,' said Coffin. 'Could be three. I wonder if Mrs Kay Zeman ate chocolate cake?'

'I am asking for an exhumation order there,' said Lane defensively.

There was a moment of uneasy silence. Both Superintendent Lane and Inspector Young thought: The Old Man knows something we don't.

'Just thinking aloud,' Coffin said. He went on: 'But don't overlook the soup. The drug could have been in the biscuits or cake in one case and in the soup in another.'

'Poisoners usually stick to one MO,' said Lane.

'This one is different.'

Coffin played with a pencil on his desk. 'It says something about the character of the murderer. Makes him someone who was free to walk in and out of the kitchens of both houses and take an opportunity when it offered.'

'He or she,' said Lane heavily.

'Doesn't sound like the Planter Estate lot. Not exactly handed the key of the house anywhere,' said Archie Young. 'But I'll take a look at them anyway. They're great at getting into places where they shouldn't.'

'Yes, I should do that,' advised the Chief Commander. 'Don't give up on anyone, because as I see it there are pointers this way and that.'

'You say so,' said Lane, half questioningly. He had the feeling that he was picking up vibrations that could shake his picture of the crime, already forming. He seemed to see Felicity Zeman as the poisoner. A kind of female vengeance figure, wiping out her husband's lover and her son like a Greek fate, dealing out her own justice.

'Think about it.' Coffin put down the pencil and stood up. The meeting was over.

As they went out, both Young and Lane had a similar thought, but it was Archie Young who got it out: 'He knows something we don't. Felt that, didn't you?' He rubbed his ankle, still sore. That bloody dog.

'He gets around far too much,' said Lane. 'Talks to people. Sees round corners.' He sounded disapproving. 'Thinks too much.' But this he did not say aloud, it would reflect on himself. Also, he owed a lot to John Coffin, and there was loyalty. He hoped the Old Man wasn't going over the top. He blamed Stella Pinero.

JOHN COFFIN had his own informant. He had established a friendship with an elderly local inhabitant, Mimsie Marker, the proprietor of the stand selling newspapers and magazines by the Spinnergate Tube Station, every morning, every day including Sundays. But Sunday she packed up at midday and went home. Wherever home was, as Mimsie kept quiet about this. She had a basement flat in Parmiloe Street, had had for years, ever since being bombed out of Woodstock Street as a young war bride. But it was generally believed she owned a large suburban house in Wimbledon where she kept either a lover or one invalid daughter, according to how your fancy took you.

She was locally famous for her hats, flowery in summer and velvety and feathery in winter. It was summer, so her hat was adorned with violets, layers of them, violets upon violets. No one ever saw her without her hat, nor knew where she found them. No ordinary hatmaker had piled those violets upon violets. Stella Pinero had said that a rose confection that only came out on high days like a royal wedding had been made by Simone Mirman in Paris, and that there was one that Rose Bertin might have created.

'But Rose Bertin made hats for Marie Antoinette,' Coffin had protested.

'And after the revolution, for Josephine too. And these are very old hats.'

A walking hat museum or not, Mimsie was always very well informed, as someone will be who spends all the day on the pavements.

She always had John Coffin's papers ready for him, although in her opinion he wasted his time reading those that had no real news in them. The only one to read was the *Thameside Times*, in which, if you read between the lines, you got all important local news. International or national stuff did not count, you watched the TV news for that, or didn't bother. Still, she was always there to inform him.

It was a pleasure as well as a duty, like Arthur and his bites, with whom, indeed, she had a lot in common: both wary Londoners, ever ready to defend themselves and their friends.

'Nasty business,' she said, as she handed over his papers. 'How's Dr Zeman?'

'Early days yet.'

'If he's not dead by now, he'll live. I knew his old dad, Dr Victor. Tough, that lot. That'll be two-fifty.'

Coffin handed the money over. 'Think so?'

'Wasn't meant for him, anyway.'

'Are you sure of that, Mimsie?'

She ignored the question. Who was sure of anything? 'You know who did it, don't you?'

'No, I don't. Surprised if you do.'

She ignored this also, nor did she answer it directly. That would be too straightforward for Mimsie. 'Know who they're saying did it?'

'Who is they?' Of course, he knew, but one had to play it Mimsie's way.

'Us, us locals. People like me who have always lived here, not the new lot.'

'So who have they picked on? I suppose there is a name?'

'Yes. They think Fred Kinver is wiping out the Zemans to avenge his daughter. And they say Good Luck to him.'

'But the Zemans have lived around here a long time too, Mimsie.'

'Makes no difference. Well off, you see.'

'And do you think Fred Kinver killed them, Mimsie?'

Mimsie just smiled, showing sparkling white false teeth.

Coffin remembered all this as he went home, late on that violent Sunday. He was hearing too much about Fred Kinver.

BOB ALWAYS demanded an evening walk, pointing out in an anxious way that without this walk his bladder could not manage to last. Once or twice he had got Stella up in the middle of the night to prove his point.

On the Sunday, when the fires were out and the streets quiet, she took him as far as Max's Delicatessen: Max never closed until midnight, even on a Sunday. She could have a drink of coffee, give Bob a biscuit, although not chocolate. The rumour about the use of chocolate to mask the presence of poison had spread through the district with great speed.

It was about nine o'clock, and a fine evening. Usually at this time, Max's was busy with people drinking coffee and eating cake, buying ice-cream or just gossiping. The Theatre Workshop crowd used it as a kind of club. Max encouraged his customers just to drop in even if they didn't buy. 'They are my friends,' he said. 'I like to see them, pass the time of day. It makes my work happy.'

It also made his till ring, because few emerged without buying something, even if it was only a packet of coffee. He sold good coffee, the best in London, he claimed.

But tonight the place was almost deserted. Just one couple sitting in a corner over glasses of iced coffee. Sir Harry Beauchamp and Dick, heads together, talking quietly. They had the reputation of being the worst old gossips in London, but without malice.

Max was on his own. 'My wife has a migraine, I have one myself. I think. It is that sort of day.'

Sir Harry looked up and waved her over. 'Come and join us. We need cheering up. I've just signed on the dotted line for the new apartment in St Luke's Mansions. We wanted to be near Dicky's gallery.' He patted Dick's hand, they made no bones about their relationship; they lived independently but each apartment had a double bed. 'And now I'm wondering if I've done the right thing.'

Stella walked across to them followed by Bob. Bob was allowed in on sufferance because he was known to be a dog of sorrows, a bereaved boy, but otherwise Max did not encourage animals.

'A double espresso, Max, please.' Stella sat down by Sir Harry. 'And a custard cream wafer for Bob.' It was better if Bob was a paying customer. 'Oh, you'll like it round here,' she said loyally. 'It's very agreeable. Usually, anyway. Perhaps it's a bit rough at the moment.' She decided not to tell him about the fire that never was in the courtyard, since he obviously did not know.

'I don't want to be savaged on my way home,' said Sir Harry. 'I keep late hours, and there's poor Dick's place. Some cad painted on his wall. Quite a nice drawing but a bit graphic.' Delicately, he said no more.

'Has he wiped it out?'

'No, it was quite decoratively done, and I'm going to photograph it for my book on graffiti.'

That book ought to be quite a sizzler, Stella thought, if all she had heard about Sir Harry's haunts were true. There was said to be a bit of rough trade down by the Dock in the Plymouth Bar, and she had heard stories about one of the local discos too. You heard every sort of gossip in the theatre world without taking it to heart. Live and let live. However, she did not usually pass on such tidbits to John Coffin, although he probably knew of them professionally. He must know of every sink and stew and den in the district.

'For private publication only, of course,' said Sir Harry, with a wicked look in his pale blue eyes.

'Of course.'

'I had to pay a pretty price for my apartment. She drives a hard bargain, your landlady. She says she needs every penny for the new theatre.'

'I expect she does.'

'And she's sister to our eminent detective.'

'Half-sister.'

'I suppose he affords us some protection.'

'You could say that.'

'On the other hand, he might attract violence,' said Dick, making a rare contribution to the conversation.

'Naughty,' said Sir Harry, slapping his hand.

Stella sipped her coffee while Bob swallowed his biscuit and looked round for more.

'I was sorry about that poor boy Zeman. He had such a lovely face.'

'You knew him?' Stella was surprised.

'Seen him around,' said Sir Harry easily. 'I notice faces. It's my job. I liked what I saw. I might have photographed him. A lot inside him.'

'Perhaps we ought to get off,' said Dick; he was said to be the jealous one.

'Give you a lift home, Stella?'

'No, I must walk. It's for Bob.'

Bob looked up at hearing his name, stood and gave a shake. Stella picked up his leash and they departed. Bob was like an old horse and only ever wanted to take the walk he knew. Now he showed a strong determination to head off in the direction of Feather Street.

Stella let him take her that way, it was a fine night, the coffee had refreshed her, and she had Bob with her, after all. What was there to be afraid of?

To her surprise, Bob went through Feather Street without more than a sniff at the odd lamp-post, then carried on briskly to the bottom of the road. Here, outside the Marsh house, he stopped and looked up hopefully.

Stella laughed. 'Obvious where Jim takes you on your walks. Home. Well, not tonight, Bob.'

She moved him on, letting him lead her round the corner and up Brazen Hill. She knew this led back to St Luke's.

But outside a house, Bob showed a desire to linger again. This time it had a big brass plate: John Dibben. Veterinary Surgeon. Obviously another of his haunts.

'Come on, Bob, nearly home now. Just a pull up the hill.'

Brazen Hill soon flattened out, turned into a busy main road and then led to St Luke's Mansions.

Stella walked in through the main doorway where all the entrances to the flats were situated. Once it had been the door of the church, but Letty Bingham's architect had opened it up in a charming way to form a small cloister.

John Coffin was just arriving in his car which seemed to have a curious dulled look as if someone had dipped it in soapy water and not polished it. Stella waved at him, pulled on by Bob, now anxious for water, and sleep.

'I'll catch you up, Stella,' called Coffin. 'Want to talk.'

Then he heard her scream.

He got out of the car and ran into the building after her. Someone had turned out the light that always shone at night, but the moon was up so he could see her.

She was staring down at a figure lying propped against the wall. She had stopped screaming but shudders were running through her.

The figure wore a man's dark old trousers, a tweed jacket and a striped cotton shirt with scarf at the neck, on the bulbous head was an old tweed cap. Black boots stuck out from the legs.

Stella still shuddered. 'He hasn't got a face,' she said.

Coffin bent down and touched. Paper stuck out from where the arms would have ended, the legs in the old boots gave under his fingers. The body was stuffed with paper, rolls and rolls of newspaper.

'It's the Paper Man,' he said. He put his arm round Stella, holding her close.

# FOURTEEN

*Sunday to Monday, June 25—26, and it rolls on through the week*

WHERE THERE SHOULD have been a face was an oval of white paper, roughly cut with jagged edges. The paper gleamed pale in the moonlight, managing to look sinister and blank at the same time.

Coffin drew Stella away. She was still hanging on to Bob's leash so he took it from her. Bob was sniffing at the dummy, growling softly under his breath at the same time. As Coffin took his leash he snapped and gave a high bark.

'Shut up, Bob.'

'Do be quiet, Bob,' said Stella in a weak voice. 'You'll wake the neighbours.' Then she started to laugh.

Coffin gave her a little shake. 'Shut up, Stella, and calm down. I am going to take you upstairs, give you a strong drink, and then you are going down to your own place with Bob and sleep well.'

'Can't I stay up there with you?' Soft little tears were beginning to appear in her eyes. 'I'd feel so much safer.'

'I've got work to do.'

'I'm coming with you,' said Stella with determination.

'Don't be silly. Shall I telephone Lily to come over?'

He poured her a large glass of whisky, sat her down on his big comfortable sofa, sat himself next to her, and watched while she drank it.

'Better now? Right, I'm taking you to your place, and I'll wait with you while you settle yourself in.'

Stella stood up. 'Stay the night?'

'No, better not. Come on.' He took her arm.

'We shall have to pass . . . that thing.'

'You needn't look. I'll lead you past.'

'I'll see, I know I will.'

'Pretend you're blind.'

She started to laugh. 'Oh, you do cheer me up. Thank you.'

They went down his turret staircase together. 'You've got this place nice, John.'

'I know.' He did know. It felt like home. He had his carpets, his pictures, not many, but collected with love, and books, plenty of those.

He put his arm round her when they got to the cloister and led her past the figure.

'Still there?' asked Stella, pausing for a moment.

'Yes, it hasn't got on a bus and travelled home.'

Stella laughed again. 'The last bus went an hour ago.' But she kept her head up and walked past bravely. 'Here I go, poor blind Stella.'

'Good girl.'

He opened her door for her and Bob nipped inside briskly. He had had enough of the night.

'Want me to come in?'

'No, I'm all right. Seen worse, after all.'

'You have.' She had once found a severed hand in her refrigerator.* He kissed her gently. They always

---

* *Coffin in the Black Museum*

kissed good night; Stella kissed everyone. But this kiss felt different.

'I do love you, John.'

'Good night, Stella.' It was better to leave it there. For the moment, anyway.

Her door closed and he heard her lock it. Then he walked over to the dummy again.

Now he was on his own, he went over to the main switch that controlled the lights in the cloister and switched it on. Then he walked back to the mannequin.

It was smaller than a man, but it had been carefully put together. Whose clothes? Bought at some charity shop, he speculated.

An unpleasing object. Hello, Paper Man. I can't say I like the look of you, but what are you doing here? What is your purpose?

Not just to frighten Stella, he thought.

But Stella had been wrong. The Paper Man had got a face. Pinned to the oval of white paper was a tiny photograph. It looked as though it had been cut out of a newspaper.

He knelt down to get a closer look. He recognized the face of Fred Kinver.

With careful fingers, he searched the pockets of jacket and trousers: they were empty. No, there was a piece of paper in one of the pockets. It was a cleaning ticket.

He took off the cap, which had rested on a stocking stuffed with newspaper. The cap went back on. The whole of the dummy would have to be gone over by the forensic people to see what they could pick up.

The jacket interested him. It had been cleaned (the charity shop would demand that before it was resold) but it was made of thick, rough tweed to which anything like strands of cotton or hair would cling. He thought he could see some fibres that had stuck to the front of the jacket.

He touched one gently with his fingernail. The small strand clung on, stickily. It was a natural fibre.

Coffin leaned back on his heels. 'Well, Paper Man, I believe you may have given away a little bit more than you think.'

THE NEXT DAY was quiet. The police put extra patrols on the street and police cars circled the area methodically, with special attention to the Planter Estate.

Named after a long dead Labour MP who had lived locally, the Planter Estate was no happy memorial to anyone.

This estate on the edge of Leathergate, running towards Spinnergate, had a bad reputation which was thoroughly well deserved, as even the inhabitants themselves recognized. Planters experienced more break-ins, more muggings, more violent assaults as well as more rapes, more incest, and more murders than any other district. Crime was its principal industry and it exported it as well.

It was an unlovely area, built some thirty years ago by a hopeful architect who had not foreseen what his bleak blocks and walkways could produce. He had not seen the crime wave coming. If he had, he would not have designed as many underground passages and rat walks as he had done. But he had got a prize for it at the time, and several subsequent contracts for similar work. The estate was due to be demolished soon by a housing authority despairing of keeping the roofs waterproof and the windows in repair. So it was to be blown up, if it didn't fall down first.

It was one of those areas in his bailiwick which gave Coffin the most trouble.

There was another but much smaller area behind the Spinnergate Tube Station, which was called Dean's Park. It was known locally as DreamLand. It was the local drug alley. Planters oddly enough did not go in for drugs so much. Its natural vitality hurled itself into straight violence in pursuit of getting what it wanted. Fights between Planters and Dreamers were a regular part of the scene. Great dogs, Alsatians, Rottweilers, Dobermans and any mix of all three, were a feature of both districts, these formed packs and fought too. To the death sometimes.

There was disagreement about whether the Planters were worse than the Dreamers, but the general police view was that the Planters were violent but were human beings while the Dreamers were animals. Opinions differed on how to handle them. Some police thought you ought to go in hard and strong and let them know you were there, while others thought you should take it all quietly and keep the level of tension low. But either way was wrong sometimes, and hot weather always made it worse. It was hot now.

At the moment both Planters and Dreamers seemed to be off the streets, although watchful local policemen reported that small numbers could be seen flitting around dark corners, which didn't look promising for peace.

THE FIGURE OF the Paper Man was taken into police custody, and might have rested in the corner of a room for ever if the Chief Commander had not issued orders that he was to be 'gone over thoroughly'. So he was taken to bits and spread out on a laboratory table. Even so, some people thought he was just a silly joke and it was a waste of time. Fred Kinver was quietly watched, but no action was taken.

The exhumation order on Mrs Kay Zeman was granted and her body removed from its grave to great public and media interest. Nothing much was happening on the international scene, so there was space to spare for crimes in Leathergate and Spinnergate. Never had Coffin more desired some great scandal or upheaval to break out elsewhere. A revolution, anywhere, would have suited him.

Very quickly, on Tuesday morning, Dr Angela Livingstone reported that she had found traces of the drug Digoxin in Kay Zeman's body. After so long, such a residue would have been hard to find if she had not known what she was looking for.

Detectives intensified their search for the source of the drug. A detective-sergeant, assisted by a squad of plain clothes detectives, men and women, was put in charge of this part of the investigation. He reported back to Archie Young, who then passed on all the reports to all interested parties, including the Chief Commander.

Dr Felicity Zeman denied having handled or used any Digoxin, she worked only in the hospital. This denial was only to be expected, and, in the view of the two officers, Superintendent Lane and Inspector Archie Young, who were handling the inquiry, meant nothing. Just what she would say.

John Coffin was inclined to believe her. He was already forming an idea about the poisoner. He could almost fit a face there.

Archie Young had spoken to the doctor at the Elmgate Health Centre himself. He knew that tact would be needed and he went there in as quiet a spirit as was possible to his naturally ebullient and forceful personality.

The Elmgate Health Centre was new and well built. The centre reception hall flashed with lights. You followed your light, just as on the London Underground or Heathrow. His light, for Dr Jeff Green, was blue.

'I know you've got to ask these question,' said Dr Green, settling back into his chair. 'And I've got not to answer. But at least I can tell you what I did not prescribe.' He was a calm-looking man whose patients trusted him.

Dr Green, who had looked after Val, was able to say that he had never prescribed the drug. Val Humberstone had low blood pressure but was not given any drugs for it. As Dr Green reported it, 'she wanted to cure herself.'

'She was having hypnotherapy, I think,' he said with a shrug. 'I didn't mind, it works for some people. She was going to a good man. Miss Humberstone had periods of feeling slightly unwell, it was entirely natural. Any symptoms she showed around the time of her death may have been due to natural causes and not the drug. That could have come later.'

'Are you suggesting,' said Archie Young, 'that the murderer deliberately chose a time when she was unwell to dose her?'

'It might have helped mask the symptoms of poisoning. Helped towards the idea of natural death.'

Young considered this thoughtfully as he left. In fact, in the case of Mrs Zeman it did do that, he thought. Earlier he had seen Kay Zeman's doctor who had been blandly unhelpful, as might have been expected of a partner of Leonard Zeman's, but who had denied prescribing Digoxin. Mrs Zeman had had a mild heart condition but had been receiving other treatment.

On the way out from seeing Jeff Green, Archie Young met one of the Planters gang, and grabbed him by his leather jacket. 'Where's your friend Slater?' Both Slater and Graham had been absent from their usual haunts for some days.

The Planter, a boy called Tinker, pulled himself away. 'No idea. Don't handle me like that. That's good gear you've got there.'

'Tell him I want him.'

'Like I said, I never see him.'

'Do it. What you are coming in here for?' He was suspicious of Tinker, every right-minded subject of the Queen would be.

'I've got a bad heart,' said Tinker with a smirk. He managed to kick Young as he wrenched himself away. His boot hit the spot where Arthur put his teeth in.

Young was furious. 'I could nick you for that.'

'Try it and see.'

But it was a hopeless encounter and Young knew it. 'Graham and Slater, I want them both. Tell them that. Or you'll want more than a doctor.' Hopeless again, he cursed himself for being stupid. It wasn't any good getting tough with Tinker, he wasn't bright enough.

As Archie Young set down his notes, he wrote, thinking about the poison: 'A conclusion: another characteristic of the murderer: an opportunist, who saw a moment and took it.'

Also means he or she was in close contact, possibly daily contact, with the victim, thought John Coffin, as he read Young's notes. But he had already decided this for himself. It had to be so.

BOTH THE KINVERS had taken their health problems to a doctor on the other side of Leathergate where it marched with Spinnergate, and he refused to discuss his patients, beyond saying he had not seen Fred Kinver for years. Mrs Kinver had been given a sedative after the death of her daughter, but she had not come back for a repeat prescription. He would have given her one. He was a one man practice and he was busy, so if the Inspector would allow...?

Archie Young felt he got nothing there, beyond a feeling that Fred Kinver was too reclusive to be true.

A general trawl round the doctors of the neighbourhood met with stiff medical resistance, as was to be expected. Records of patients were private and confidential and nothing could be disclosed.

A check on the pharmacists was more successful. They were willing to provide statistics, at least.

Young was gloomy when he saw the figures, brought in by his sergeant, Frank Reilly. 'Half the district must be on it by the look of these tables. Well, we'll have to go underground a bit. Take the chemists nearest to Feather Street.' He looked at a map of the area. 'Only four, and Boots is one, we know they lost no Digoxin in their break-in, but see what you can pry out of one of the assistants. Not ethical, but have a go.' Frank Reilly was a nice-looking man, at present unmarried after an early divorce. 'Do it yourself, Frank, see what you can get. Try all three other shops. We have to find out how and who could lay hands on this drug.'

If this was a real village, he thought, as people are always saying we are, then we'd know who was on the drug. Someone would have told us.

IN SPITE OF WHAT had looked like promising leads, a time of stalemate in both cases, the murder of Anna Mary Kinver and the Zeman poisonings, had set in. They were at that time when both cases could go dead for ever and no one ever be charged. It might be that the police could make guesses, but proof might be hard to come by. In these two cases everyone was making different guesses. Felicity Zeman, poisoner-in-chief? Tim Zeman, rapist and murderer? Fred Kinver, what?

Stalemate it might have been, but the Paper Man stepped in. He sent out another letter. This went out to a carefully selected group, as if the Paper Man knew whom he wanted to talk to. One went to the Chief Commander at his home address in St Luke's Mansions, one went to Superintendent Lane, and another to inspector Archie Young. A fourth was dropped on Mimsie Marker's stall, she didn't know how but was highly diverted to have one. And one more was pinned on Felicity Zeman's gatepost in Feather Street. The make-up was the same as before, letters cut from newspapers or magazine, but the execution was getting sloppier, perhaps because the Paper Man was now writing so many letters.

*Thought you'd seen the last of me, did you? Got one more to go then I've done the lot. Ta-ta for now.*

To the police it looked like a confession of murder. It also seemed like a threat.

THE LETTER STUCK ON the Zeman house was seen by Jim Marsh who had two dogs with him, Bob and Arthur. These two, although not exactly friends, would strike up a polite comradeship in the interests of a good walk, unlike the pair of Jack Russells for whom it would have been a fight to the death.

Jim looked at the letter, decided now the time had come, removed it, put it in his pocket and went round to the big new police station. Here, he asked to see the Chief Commander, John Coffin.

He had the name pat, and rolled it off briskly.

The man on duty behind the desk was interested and amused, but said: 'Sorry. He's busy.'

Jim was prepared for this. 'Superintendent Lane will do, then.' Then he added: 'For the time being.'

The constable was just about to open his mouth to say No can do, laddie, when he met Jim's eyes and decided that this was not the boy to call laddie. 'He's busy too,' he contented himself with. 'But tell me what it is and I'll do what I can.'

'Inspector Young, then,' said Jim, sitting down. The dogs sat too. 'I'll wait. I'm not kidding.'

'Inspector Young is busy too.'

'I'll write a note.' He stood up, took a notebook from his pocket and upon a page wrote a message which he then tore out. 'Give it to him, please.' And then, because the constable still stood there. 'He'll want to see it, you know. It's your head on the block.'

There was something about Jim that convinced the constable that if his head was indeed on the block, Jim would be the one to use the axe. 'See what I can do,' he said.

He read the note on his way down the passage, which Jim had intended he should do.

Addressed to Inspector Young it said simply: *I am going to tell you who the Paper Man is*.

Not, the constable noticed, I want to tell you, or I can tell you, but straight out: I am going to tell you.

Shout it from the rooftops, most like, the constable said to himself. He decided it was entirely in character with what he had seen of Jim Marsh.

The message found its way on to Archie Young's desk at last and he read it.

'I'm in a good mood today,' he said. 'I'll talk to the boy. But let him wait. If he waits long enough, then I'll see.'

An hour later, Jim was waiting.

Two hours later, he was still there.

Three hours later, he was there.

At four o'clock in the afternoon Jim got in to see the Inspector. He took the dogs with him.

In the interval, the constable on the desk, who had a conscience, had given Jim a cup of tea and the dogs several bowls of water. The reception area now smelt strongly of mongrel and peke. At four, the constable went off duty, sneezing, having discovered he had an allergy to dogs.

Young said: 'Well, lad, what can I do for you?'

'I'll need to have the Superintendent here. I'd like the Chief Commander as well, but the Superintendent will do.'

'I'm glad to hear that.'

'No, you're not. You think I'm stupid. I'm not and I'm not playing games. I could behave quite differently. Tell someone else, the BBC or a newspaper. But I want to do this properly. I have something to show you. And I need a witness. I'm protecting myself.'

He looked capable of staying in Young's office all night if he had to, dogs and all.

'Tell me what it is you want to show me. If it's worth my while, I'll send a man down with you.'

'No. I know you lot. If you don't like what I show you, or it doesn't fit in, then you'll lose it. Accidentally on purpose.'

'I can see you've got a high opinion of us.'

'Yes, that's why I want the boss there. I trust him.'

Jim was beginning to feel desperate, which accounted for the tartness of his tongue. This was not going how he wanted it. It was so important and this fool did not see it.

Archie Young took a chance. 'Look, come with me. This is about the Paper Man, you think he's important. So do I. I'll let you have a look at our Major Incident Room where you can see how seriously we take the Paper Man, and the murder of Anna Mary Kinver. Yes, I can see that interests you. And we've just set up a room for the Zeman poisonings. The two rooms will be in touch with each other. Perhaps you will trust me then.'

Jim stood up. If this was all he was going to get, so be it. But he hadn't parted with his information yet.

'Must the dogs come?'

'Yes.' It was take it or leave day.

'All right. Then when you've had a look, you can tell me what you've got. Or you can go home.'

On the stairs on the way to Miriam Room, they met John Coffin, on his way in.

Bob leapt forward with a joyful bark. A friend, he was shouting, someone who will get me out of this boring building where the smells are uninteresting.

'WHY ARE YOU so much nicer to me than that other policeman?' demanded Jim Marsh suspiciously. He was leading the way through the streets. He was carrying Arthur who would walk no further. Bob had attached himself to John Coffin. 'You're coming with me like this, letting me show you what I've got. Well, not got myself,' he corrected. 'But know where something is you ought to see. Something I have found.'

'Perhaps I've got a bit more time.'

'But you're the boss man. You ought to be busier.'

There was a lot of truth in this, so Coffin did not answer directly. Sharp boy, he thought, sharp tongue.

'I'm interested,' he said. 'And I think it might be important. I thought something would have to turn up. Be found, as you put it. That in itself would be important.'

'Think so?' Jim sounded intrigued.

'It's how I see it.'

'Is that how cases are solved?'

'Not really. Mostly by hard work and attention to detail. With a bit of luck.'

'Am I the luck?'

'You could be.'

'I believe in luck,' said Jim. 'But I think you have to make things happen too. Or believe in them enough to make them happen.'

'That probably is the recipe for a successful career,' said Coffin.

'Oh, I wasn't thinking of a career. I won't have one. We don't in our family,' said Jim, putting his head down and plodding on. After a few more moments, he said: 'You haven't asked where we're going.'

'Bob seems to know,' Coffin looked down at Bob, who was straining at his leash.

'Might do. Got a good memory for a dog.'

'Haven't they all?'

'Depends. Like human beings, some are better than others.'

Coffin looked up at the sky. 'I flew over this whole area in a helicopter when I first came here. To see what I'd got. You'd be surprised at the things you see. Not as densely inhabited as you think. Plenty of green, parks, allotments, bits of open land. Pathways, tracks, they stand out.'

Jim led the way in a confident manner round a corner, down one more short side-street and then across the road to where a patch of open land by the railway embankment near to Brazen Head Docks had been made over to allotments, most with small sheds.

He said nothing but went straight across to one of the more battered-looking constructions. It had a thick old door but the lock looked useless. Here he stopped, turned round and faced Coffin. 'This is it. We're here.'

Coffin stood back and surveyed the area. The allotment had not received much attention lately, not in the way of gardening. 'Who does it belong to?'

'Fred Kinver.'

Might have guessed, thought Coffin. 'Well? What are we here for?'

'It's what's inside. What I've found.'

'By chance?' inquired Coffin sceptically.

'No, I was looking. I thought I'd find something. I've been watching Fred Kinver. He's mad, you know.'

Jim pushed open the door. He knew how to do it. Coffin followed him in. The room was dark, the small window blocked by boxes of seedlings struggling for the light.

'Ought to get those tomatoes planted out,' said Jim, in a disapproving voice. 'Still, it's not what he's been thinking about.'

'And what has he been thinking about?'

'Have a guess.' Jim was busy pulling at a cardboard box hidden amongst some seed catalogues on a table. He laid it in front of Coffin. 'Here, take a look.'

Bob and Arthur settled themselves on the earth floor as if they knew the ropes and knew they would have to be patient.

'Does Mr Kinver know you make yourself free of his shed?' Coffin was opening the box. Inside were two large notebooks, the sort you can buy at any newsagent's or stationer's.

Jim laughed. 'What do you think?'

One book was labelled *A Murder. Anna Mary Kinver*. Coffin turned the pages slowly. On each page were pasted cuttings from newspapers and magazines. Each was concerned with the killing. Fred Kinver must have had his scissors into all the dailies and periodicals over the last few months. He had even got his hands on French, German and Italian papers. The library was going to be angry when it found out what it had lost.

A man with an obsession, Coffin thought. One he was feeding with rich nourishment.

The second book was labelled *The Police*. But in fact it was filled with the life, as far as could be culled from the newspapers, of John Coffin. Kinver had even managed to seize some cuttings from earlier cases of years ago.

Coffin had to admire the man's industry. As he looked at blurred pictures of himself in his twenties, he understood that this was an extension of the original obsession. Whether it was a sign of healing or an aggravation, he could not be sure. A psychiatrist seemed called for.

He leafed through them slowly. Finally, he said. 'Well, thanks for showing me.'

'Ah, that's not it.' Jim was amused. 'All you see there is just a cover-up. Something to explain what he was doing down here. If he had to. I'll show you the real stuff.'

He pulled an old chest of drawers which had been used to store seeds, catalogues and bits of garden equipment away from the wall, then he knelt down and lifted a bit of old carpet which rested on boards. Jim pulled at the boards. They came up at once, revealing a hole. At the bottom of the hole was a small tin trunk.

Jim lifted it out. Inside was a battered portable typewriter and folder of papers. A strong smell of disinfectant came with it, making him wonder what had been stored in it originally.

Coffin looked at the typewriter in surprise.

'Bought at a charity shop, I'd say,' summed up Jim judicially.

'Can Fred Kinver type?' Coffin was already studying the papers, all covered with typed passages. Blocks of passages. All dated. It seemed to be a kind of diary.

'One-finger stuff. You can tell when you look.'

'You have looked, of course?'

'Sure. Now you, it's your turn.'

John Coffin read:

### DEATH NUMBER ONE. Two days after Anna Mary's death.

I know now that Anna Mary is dead. This was hard to accept at first. I don't think her mother has done yet. She seems too calm. I am not calm, there is an explosive feeling inside me, like a fire, like a volcano, I know I am full of energy that must burst out. How I did not know at first, but now I know what I am going to do, because I know what I am. I was not a good father, I admit it, I am guilty there, but I can clear my guilt.

Justice. I am the hand of Justice.

Day Three After. I do not say after what, because I cannot write it any more. Too much pain.

I know what I should do. First I must become another person. If I am me, then I cannot act freely. As a new person, I am above the law.

Day Three After, the night.

God has told me how to become another person. I am to do it by writing. I shall write letters, letting people know there is a person out there. I must not let myself be revealed until my work is done, so my letters must be carefully prepared. There need not be many. A few will establish me.

Now diary, I can tell you what I mean to do. God has told me to write it out. He tells me it will ease my pain. Nothing can ease Anna Mary's pain. I don't believe she has gone to any other and happier world. Her mother does believe this. Or perhaps she just pretends. We are both doing a lot of pretending. But not here, diary, you know my true heart and intention. I prepared the first letter yesterday. Shall I send it out? Is the time right? I know what I have done. It is not hard to kill, not if your cause is just.

Justice is mine, says the Lord. Or is that Vengeance? Same thing, very often. Anyway, he hands the job out to us humans. Has to. Only reasonable.

I have done one job.

Over a week since Anna Mary was killed.

I can't think in days any more. They seem to run together. Sent off a letter.

My letter got good publicity. The police wanted to keep it quiet but it got out.

Did another job.

THERE WERE several more entries on the same lines.

Another job, an entry read. Two, three, if it works. Then it is over. I have done. Jobs jobbed.

Dangerous stuff, Coffin thought.

At the end of the book a copy of one of the Paper Man letters was pasted in. He saw that with interest. He had half expected it to be there.

The diary of the Paper Man was in his hands, complete with a confession of identity. Well, more or less. Found where it was, there could not be much doubt.

Fred Kinver, the Paper Man and multiple poisoner.

He looked up to meet Jim's curious gaze. 'Read it all?'

'As much as I can at the moment.'

'You don't seem surprised.'

'I think I had the feeling that something like this was about to happen. You get to a point in a case when that feeling comes.'

'What gives you that feeling?'

'Hard work and attention to detail,' said Coffin drily.

'Not luck?'

'The luck is when the feeling happens.' Coffin's voice was quiet and cool.

'I reckon I'm your luck.'

'You didn't happen on these papers by chance, Jim, did you?'

''Course not. I've been watching him. I get lots of chances, out with the dogs.'

'I wonder he didn't see you were watching.'

'Oh, he's well away, I can tell you. Anyway, I was careful. I found these papers last night. Knew they must be there, so I hunted around. But I needed someone I could trust to show them to. Didn't want anyone getting the wrong ideas.'

'Let's get the papers back where they were, Jim. I'll give you a hand. Then I'll send someone down to collect them.' Archie Young and posse, probably, they would enjoy the job.

'Shall I stay and guard them?' asked Jim with enthusiasm.

'No. I don't think that's going to be necessary. No one's going to steal them.'

'Fred might come down and remove them.'

'I don't think so.'

They emerged into the open air of the allotments. Several gardeners gave them interested looks, but nothing was said.

'I suppose Fred will be arrested now?'

Coffin did not answer.

'Well, he deserves punishing. And what about me? Will I get a reward?'

'I don't think there is one, Jim, but I promise to do what's right for you.' As they left the allotments, he said: 'Better get home with the dogs.'

WHEN HE GOT BACK to his office, he passed on what had been discovered to the investigating team.

'I want that boy,' said Archie Young promptly. 'Where is he now, sir?'

'Gone home with the dogs. He won't run away; he's too pleased with himself. Hoping to get his picture in the papers, I think.'

'I'll get the stuff collected, sir.' Young was excited. 'While you were away, some information came in that clinches it. Fits in with what you've found. A WPC doing the rounds of the chemists' shops had the luck to come across an assistant who was at school with her. This girl was willing to talk and she came across with the information that Mrs Kinver had a prescription for Digoxin. It was a repeat prescription. Her GP is a one man band and known to be a bit casual. One way and another she's collected a fair supply of tablets. It's all there in the records.'

'That's interesting.'

'Isn't it? So we've got our source for the poison. We know the motive: revenge for his daughter and we've more or less got a confession, I'd say, although not one Kinver expected us to read.'

'I'm not sure about that,' said Coffin. 'I think it was written to be read.'

Archie Young stuck to his point. 'I reckon we've got enough, one way and another, to bring in both the Kinvers.'

Coffin said: 'It had better be done. But I don't like it.'

It was a hot day and getting hotter.

Young sitting at his desk felt the heat rising around his feet as if he was on fire. He was still limping.

'I know what you mean,' he said. 'It won't be popular. Since Anna Mary was killed those two have been kind of local saints. And now we're bringing them in, when we haven't cleared up their daughter's murder. Some people will say that Fred Kinver was only doing what was right. We'll handle it very carefully, sir. Later tonight, I'll go round to them myself.'

But later that day was too late.

When the police drove around as quietly and discreetly as they could, Fred Kinver, met them at the door with a shotgun. Unlicensed, unlawful and highly dangerous.

'Try to take me,' he shouted, 'and I'll kill my wife first, then myself.'

And to prove he had the means, he fired a shot in the air.

A state of siege was declared.

# FIFTEEN

*Wednesday evening, June 28, before dark*

'DO YOU THINK he means it?' asked Archie Young.

The Chief Commander, and Inspector Young and Superintendent Lane were standing together, consulting with the Chief Superintendent of the uniformed branch. They were in front of the Kinver house and were visible to anyone looking from a window of that house.

They were not alone, the police were gathered in force around the Kinver home. Further down the road a police van with full radio and telephone communications was stationed, and tucked away round the corner was a vanful of armed policemen. Several armed men had already been placed at points of vantage on roofs or at nearby windows to cover as much as possible of the house. Round the back, in the garden, two men lay hidden in the bushes. All this had been done very quietly but at great speed.

Completely out of sight were two ambulances.

Beyond this again, and prevented by a police cordon from coming closer, was a crowd of onlookers and pressmen.

'Do you think he'd really do it?' said Archie again.

'Certain of it,' returned Coffin. He hadn't liked the note in Fred Kinver's voice at all.

The Chief Superintendent started to move his feet restlessly. Lane took this for a sign of tension, which it may or may not have been.

'We can't let him kill any more people,' he said.

'I have the greatest confidence in Inspector Lee,' said the head of the uniformed branch. 'He's had a lot of experience, he was down at the Docks when the SS *Athena* was under siege. He knows what to do. He knows what to say.'

'But Kinver isn't talking.'

'He will in the end. This is what it's all about: watching and trying and trying again.'

All three men were aware of the Chief Commander's presence and wishing he was safely tucked up in bed, or in New York, or in Brussels, anywhere but here.

Lane, although no longer as close to the man as he had been once, still read him better than the others. He's not with us on this, he thought. He's seeing things differently. He had known that to happen in the past with Coffin, and it always meant something explosive in the air. He remained watchful of his boss as well as the Kinver house: you needed four eyes in this business.

Coffin stayed quiet. He too had been on these watches before and knew how to conserve his energies. He did not think Fred Kinver was murderous tonight, but he might very well be suicidal.

'Is Fellaton coming down?' Fellaton was the Home Office psychiatrist called in on these occasions.

'Yes, sir. Lee asked for him at once. He's on his way over. He was at the Barbican at a concert so he hasn't got too far to come.'

Far enough. Long enough, it seemed to those wait-ing as the time passed and Kinver did not appear or answer his telephone.

When Professor Fellaton appeared, wearing a dark suit and looking serious, he gave the quartet a bare nod and passed on to the radio car.

'Hope he gets on with it,' said Lane gloomily. 'The longer it lasts, the worse it'll be.'

'Not necessarily,' said John Coffin. He made his way over to Fellaton, a man he had met once before and on a similar occasion. A young man had shut himself and his young wife into his caravan, threat-ening to shoot them both if an attempt was made to arrest her. She was wanted for shoplifting. Professor Fellaton had concluded that she had sought arrest in order to escape from her violent husband. That epi-sode had ended well, although the marriage, presum-ably, had not.

'Anything you want,' he said to Fellaton, 'just let me know. Any back-up you need.'

'Let you know.' Fellaton's famous gruff manner was well in evidence. 'I've been briefed. Expect to man-age. Ought to be able to talk him down.' He was not precisely an optimist but he was a professional: he knew what he could achieve.

Coffin stayed for a while, then returned to the trio of watchers. They had now withdrawn to the shelter of a tree where mugs of coffee were being handed round.

Coffin took his mug, moving a few paces apart to lean against the comfortable tree-trunk. He remem-bered once, during that long-ago war, finding com-fort in an air raid in the feel of the bark of a tree. It had smelt of continuing life and warmth in the face of

a situation of considerable alarm and tension. He felt
that way now; he needed to think.

Presently his eye caught a movement at one of the
windows of the Kinver house. Fred Kinver threw open
the window and appeared in the opening.

'Here we go,' said Archie Young's voice behind him.

Fred Kinver was shouting something, the words
difficult to hear. Professor Fellaton slowly came forward.

'Now you lot keep quiet,' he said. 'Leave it to me
and Jack Lee.'

As Coffin watched the scene, saw Fred waving and
shouting from the window, heard the quiet voice of
Lee relayed on speaker urging Fred to calm down and
take his time, they had all the time in the world, a
uniformed constable touched his arm. 'Sorry to interrupt, sir, but there's a call come through for you.'

THE NEWS HE HEARD was bad: two gangs of youths,
the Planters and the Dreamers, had appeared on the
streets and were on the rampage. Windows had been
broken, cars overturned, fires started in the gutters
and left to burn. The fire brigade had been called out
to two incidents already, others could be expected.
One man injured, he had a broken leg, a woman had
been burnt rescuing her cat.

In addition, in what appeared to be a spontaneous
but separate movement, the district of East Spinnergate which touched Leathergate down by Rope Alley
was putting on its own passive but determined dem-
onstration in favour of Fred Kinver. Citizens were
flooding on to the streets, milling around, not yet aggressive, but angry. At any moment the whole scene
could erupt.

As the evening went on, the gangs of Planters and Dreamers split into smaller groups. One group of Dreamers broke into Boots the Chemists again in search of drugs that they could inject, sniff or drink. Four youths from Planters stole a car and drove themselves round the streets and then turned towards St Luke's Mansions. They were singing as they went. Stella Pinero heard the singing.

From the car stationed in Elder Street, Coffin had sent a message summoning the Chief Superintendent of the uniformed branch and they had gone back to the police headquarters to take control. Reserve units were called in, and a flying squad got ready to rush to crisis spots. Additional men were held back to be used as needed.

It was all according to long-prepared plans. Coffin and Chief Superintendent Ward knew what had to be done and got on with it. For the moment, restoring the civil peace of East Spinnergate and preventing disorder spreading to Leathergate and Swinehouse and East Hythe must come first.

Inspector Lee and the Professor were dealing with Fred Kinver and already the message had come back that it was going to be a long night.

In the course of the evening, having toured the disaffected area, Coffin went back to his office. He read all the reports of the action that were arriving on his desk. He had done all that could be done, now it was his part to be the still, controlling centre.

He drank some coffee. It was daylight outside, not much past the longest day of the year.

On his table was the preliminary report on the Paper Man for which he had asked from the Forensic

Department. He pulled it towards him. It might make interesting reading.

He sat there, reading, while Stella was hearing the singing outside. She could not pick out the words, but she did not like the voices.

Presently his secretary, one of the lay assistants, came in with a fresh supply of coffee. She had a serious look on her face.

'Good of you to come in. Aren't you supposed to be on leave?'

'I felt I ought to be here, sir, with all this going on,' she said gravely. Her long thin face seemed to drop several inches. 'Must face it together.'

Coffin took some more coffee. 'We don't have a revolution on our hands, Edith, although we may yet have a riot.'

She nodded her head in a doleful fashion. 'There's a lot of sympathy for Fred Kinver. Oh, by the way, the material from the Pedloe Street Allotments has been collected. A message came in while you were out.'

'Have any trouble, did they?'

'I believe there was a bit of obstruction, but nothing to stop them.' She hesitated. 'I don't know the details, although there's talk about a diary, a sort of confession, wasn't it, sir? Feelings are mixed about the poisonings but there's a lot of sympathy for the reason behind it.'

Coffin took his coffee to the window. He could hear a police siren and then an ambulance.

'I wonder if they would feel so sympathetic if they had read that diary?' he said aloud.

Edith looked puzzled. 'You mean . . . not someone to sympathize with?'

'I think that diary shows a devious and cunning mind at work.'

'Sir?'

'Practical, too. Full of revenge, oh yes, and malice and hate.'

Edith looked frightened, as if what she had heard was something she would prefer not to understand. 'I'll take the dirty cup. Would you like me to bring in a sandwich or two?' Her instincts were always those of a kind nanny.

'Yes, later, please.'

'Ham or cheese? Or beef?'

'Anything you like.'

Coffin drew towards him the report on top of the pile. It was the forensic report on the dummy of the Paper Man. He had asked for it to be rushed through and accordingly this had been done. For once, he thought sourly.

He ran his eye over it. Almost at once, his gaze fell on a passage about the contact traces. A criminal is at risk the minute he or she touches anything.

A jacket worn by the dummy had been recently cleaned and there was a chemical residue to prove it. But in the pockets were minute shreds of tobacco together with flecks of paper, all of which had survived the cleaners. It looked as though the original owner had been a smoker who rolled his own cigarettes.

But on the front of the jacket were vegetable traces, probably from leaves, so perhaps he had been a gardener too. Also on the front of the jacket were hairs. These had been identified as dog hairs. Grey, white, and tan. These hairs, distributed over the front of the jacket, bore no sign of having been subjected to cleaning fluids and so might be presumed to come from the person who had put together the dummy.

There were plenty of dogs around, of course, thought Coffin. The Planter Estate and Dreamland were full of dogs, not to mention Feather Street.

He drank some more coffee. In No. 13 Elder Street, a siege was going on, because Fred Kinver, on what looked like solid evidence, was about to be arrested for the poisoning of the Zemans. In Leathergate and East Spinnergate there was civil disorder because a lot of his fellow citizens thought he was guilty but justified.

No sooner do you get a case set up in what looks like concrete, thought Coffin, than it begins to crack apart. I've seen it happen time and time again.

His telephone rang. He expected it to be either Lane or Young reporting on the siege in Elder Street. Over, he hoped. Or else Chief Superintendent Ward telling him the streets were quiet. Judging by the noise he could hear through his open window, this did not seem likely.

In St Luke's Mansion, Stella Pinero heard the singing stop.

The voice on the telephone for John Coffin was that of Dr Angela Livingstone from her office in Leathergate.

She sounded nervous. 'Sorry to bother you.'

I hope you won't be, thought Coffin. He made a noncommittal noise.

'I tried to get hold of Superintendent Lane or Inspector Young but they are not available.'

'Occupied with other things.'

'I can imagine.' She had got over her nerves and was speaking with more confidence. 'Look, I've heard about what is happening in Elder Street... Of course,

I don't know what evidence you've got, but there's something I ought to tell you. I ought to have drawn attention to it earlier'—But I do find Lane obnoxious and this obscured my judgement. She did not, however, offer this excuse aloud. 'The Digoxin tablets of which I found traces were blue in colour. They are more normally yellow. It can, of course be given in injections. Pediatricians use it that way.'

'So?'

'I think therefore that these tablets were a proprietary brand, much used in veterinary work.'

'You mean they are given to dogs?'

'That's right, though other animals have it, too. But it is in wide use for animals.'

'Thank you,' said Coffin. He put the telephone down.

The crack in the case had widened.

HE WENT BACK to the window. The air seemed quieter, which might be a good sign. He returned to the telephone and asked to speak to Inspector Lee in the radio van.

'How are things?'

'No strong developments as such, but Kinver is talking. He might let his wife out. He's half suggested it.'

'Would that be a good idea?'

'Depends. Might mean he's going to give up. Or might mean he's thinking of killing himself.'

Coffin considered the situation. He ought to be in two places, if not three, at once, but he had to choose. He knew without much thought what his choice would be.

'I'm going to be out of touch for a little while,' said Coffin. 'You can always reach Ward, and you have plenty of back-up.'

'Right, sir.'

'There is something I have to do.' *And I want to do it myself.*

His code name was WALKER and he was known to take tours around his own territory. Unobtrusively dressed, walking fast, he liked to see for himself.

Before he left, he managed to talk to Chief Superintendent Ward, who reported that he thought he had things under control, though you could never be quite sure what would break out, but he didn't need the troops in just yet. A gang of the Planters was on the loose but he'd soon have them. He sounded confident.

But then he always did, thought Coffin, as he walked on soft feet downhill towards Feather Street, it was what had brought him promotion, but it was not always justified.

The summer sky was beginning to darken but it was by no means night yet. He walked down Feather Street, which was quiet, and turned into the front garden of the house where the Marshes, father and son lived. He had a hope that Jim was at home, a light shone from the hall.

Jim himself opened the door. He looked startled to see his visitor.

'Are you on your own, Jim?'

'Dad's upstairs. He's asleep. He said he'd seen all the riots and demos he wanted and was tired.'

'It was you I wanted. I want you to tell me which vet the Zeman dogs were sent to.'

'Mr Dibbin. Just round the corner from here.'

'Is he home?'

Jim shrugged.

'Take me there.'

'What, me?'

'Yes, you, Jim.'

'Well, I hope he's sober,' said Jim with philosophy.

John Dibbin was indeed sober. Coffin wondered if Jim had maligned him. He had already decided not to believe all Jim told him. An inventive mind there.

He introduced himself and asked for a word in private. 'In your consulting room?' There was a strong smell of disinfectant and dog in the hall, not unpleasant but individual, a smell you would know again. 'You wait here, Jim.'

Jim, standing outside heard nothing of what went on inside. After a bit, he put his ear to the door. He heard Coffin say:

'So you are, in fact, casual about how many tablets you hand out? And consequently, how many you have lost.'

Jim giggled. You could say that again.

The door opened and Coffin appeared. 'Don't go, Jim.' He took a grip on Jim's arm. 'We'll walk together. You heard that, did you?'

'Just that last bit.' Jim strode forward, up the hill to Feather Street. 'It's just the last bit of proof you needed, isn't it. Fred used to do odd jobs down there. I suppose he helped himself to the Digoxin. And the tin trunk, smelt like Mr Dibbin, didn't it, that trunk?'

'Possibly. You seem to have heard a lot.'

Jim slowed down. 'Well, maybe I listened to a bit more than I said. Still, it's where Fred got the stuff.'

'He could have done,' said Coffin, 'if he'd wanted to, or needed to. In fact, his wife had a supply.'

'Oh. I didn't know that.'

'But I don't think he used the drug from either source. In fact, I don't believe he used anything.'

'Oh.' Jim sounded shocked. 'But the diary, what about that? And the letters?'

'He didn't write those. Oh yes, he collected those cuttings about me, that was the genuine Fred Kinver effort, but the rest . . . a fabrication, Jim, by someone too clever by half. You can tell a lot of things from forensic evidence, which often contradicts what you get from other sources. Dogs' hair on a jacket on a dummy. Hairs from dogs like Arthur and Bob. But the most valuable evidence is what you see for yourself. I told you how I went in a helicopter over all this place. I saw then all the little paths and tracks across the Feather Street gardens, and I thought: Anyone who wanted to could get from any one of those houses and into the back door of another. Quite a little network of communication to anyone who had the freedom of them. I saw that myself.'

'Well, good for you,' said Jim cockily.

'And I also saw your face down at the allotments when you got out that box. You were pleased. Too pleased with yourself, Jim, and not quite clever enough. The person who finds a box like that is likely to be the person who put it there.'

They had stopped under a tree in Feather Street, Jim with his back to it.

'You were the Paper Man, Jim, you made up the dummy and put Kinver's diary in the shed. You wrote that diary. It was your style, not his, and you betrayed yourself with every sentence. Too clever, Jim. It was all too clever, poisoning the Zemans, one by one, in their own food. I don't suppose they noticed you coming and going. And I'm told you're a fair cook. If a lethal one. I'm not sure yet in what food you put the poison, but I guess chocolate pudding, chocolate cake and chocolate biscuits, because chocolate would hide the taste and colour. And perhaps you put a touch in the gazpacho soup as well. It was your luck that the Zemans took your chocolate pudding out of the freezer that night, and Dr Felicity's luck that she only had time for a spoonful of soup. No, don't run, Jim.' Coffin reached out an arm and gripped him. 'We have a police car following us. I took that precaution.'

'They deserved it,' screamed Jim, losing control. 'Fred Kinver was a rotten father to Anna, he didn't deserve her. And Tim Zeman killed her, I know he did, or as good as. I was there. And the rest of that rotten family would have got him off. I would have done for the lot if my father hadn't got there too soon. I wish I'd poisoned him as well, and I would have done if I could have, I know he did for my mother. I hate them all.' He took a deep breath. 'And I found Anna, remember that, I found Anna Mary, I saw what she looked like, heard what she said, it was him, Zeman, that gave me a right.'

A dark car drew up to the kerb. Coffin pushed Jim in. 'Get in. I'll deal with this in my way and in my own time.' He was without sympathy: he was aware of a thick band of anger inside him. Jim Marsh deserved whatever was waiting for him. He was no killer from a sense of justice, just a killer.

On the car telephone he spoke to the radio car in Elder Street and instructed the unit there to call across to Fred Kinver that he was not suspected of mass poisoning.

'That ought to bring him in quietly.'

A report awaited him when he got back to his office from Chief Superintendent Ward that all was quietening down nicely.

All quiet.

Quiet for Stella Pinero too. The quietness of being shut up in a room with someone of whom she was terrified.

# SIXTEEN

*Wednesday in darkness*

STELLA PINERO had the local radio station on so that she heard all the news about the siege and the trouble on the streets down where Leathergate and Spinnergate ran together, a rough area, but it all seemed distant from St Luke's Mansions. She was concerned about the Kinvers, however, and was wondering what she could do to help. Not very much at the moment certainly, but afterwards... If there was an afterwards, but there must be. She was fond of Elsie Kinver and even Fred wasn't too bad when you got to know him. Off his head at the moment, obviously, and she could understand how he got there, but not a killer.

Behind her surface anxieties about who was the poisoner rested a disquiet she was not admitting. She felt vulnerable in St Luke's Mansions. Silly, perhaps, the product of an over-lively imagination, but there it was. She was frightened.

It was a hot night but she went round the rooms closing all the windows.

In the kitchen she made a pot of tea and took it back into the sitting-room where Bob snored comfortably on the sofa. Nothing in the world was going to stop him climbing on to any soft spot he took a fancy to bed down on. They would have to come to terms with each other on that.

A new play was just coming into repertory tonight, a lightweight piece, *Abigail's Party*, in which her part was small, a short run, before they heaved themselves into *Cavalcade*, so she was home early and glad to be.

She thought she was glad to be, she had fully intended to be glad, but suddenly she missed the hurly-burly of the theatre. People, voices, laughter, and movement. She could go back, almost everyone was probably still there as Lily Goldstone was having what she called a bash to celebrate a notable victory of some left-wing sort. Stella had been invited but had excused herself, she couldn't always take Lily in her radical moods.

Cup in hand, she wandered round. Nearly two years now she had lived in this flat in the adapted old church, and she had been happy. It felt more like home than some of the places she had lived in; Stella had been a bit of a wanderer.

She might stay here, dig herself in. The main theatre was slowly making its appearance. The foundations were drying out and the shape of the auditorium was now visible. Not exactly a theatre-in-the-round, you could hardly have that in what had been a church, but a theatre in the middle of a cross. The acoustics were fine, but they owed that to the original Victorian builders, who had liked a good sermon and intended every word to be audible.

The thought of John Coffin as her neighbour floated to the top of her mind, to be dealt with firmly and pushed back underneath. Their relationship was not going as she might have wished it. In the past, she had always called the tune. Now she was the uncertain one. The hopeful but might be disappointed one. The idea stung.

The radio interrupted its music with a brisk sentence about traffic diversions around Spinnergate Tube Station. The road was blocked. No explanation, just the advice to go round it, through back streets if you could.

One of those would be Rope Alley if you were on foot, thought Stella, not liking what she heard. It meant trouble.

Suddenly St Luke's Mansions did not seem so remote after all. She opened her door, went out into the little quadrangle on to which all the doors opened to listen. Sir Harry was not in residence yet, more was the pity.

She could hear the usual hum of traffic, the distant howl of a police car siren, and was that an ambulance or a fire-engine? But it was all some way off.

Stella was going back inside when she heard the singing. She could not hear the words, just as well probably, but the singing was rough. Not exactly a male voice choir. On the move too, a carload of drunks, she decided, but coming this way.

She went back to her flat, putting the chain on the door. Bob still slumbered, with an occasional twitch accompanied by a tiny growl as he dreamt. Stella gave him a pat as she passed on her way to the kitchen for more tea, but he only rolled an eye at her and refused to come awake.

Stella had changed into jeans and a silk shirt when she came in. Then she had felt hot, but now she wasn't sure if she felt hot or cold. A shiver ran through her.

Somehow the kitchen window had been left open, so she closed it. The sound of singing was nearer now. Still moving, though.

She frowned. The carload was circling the block. Going round and round, she could tell from the sound pattern. It was closer again now. She found she could almost hear the words of the song. Only it wasn't a song. If she hadn't known it was madness, she would have thought that what they were singing was: *Stella, Stella, we're coming to get you.*

A nursery nightmare, she told herself, of course they aren't singing about you. You are preoccupied with yourself, Stella, a bad fault. 'That's right, nanny,' she said. 'Stella is a silly girl.'

Stella had never had a nanny but would have welcomed a nagging but reassuring presence at that moment. She was full of unease, the tension of the whole district seeping into her spirit. Flesh, bones, nerves were all reacting.

She could telephone John Coffin. But no, she wouldn't. She couldn't add to his burdens at the moment. Anyway, she knew whom she'd get if she called his office: Edith or Will, his two guardian secretaries. A wife could break through that cordon, a Stella Pinero could not.

Perhaps a gin and tonic would do the trick. Or whisky. Everyone said whisky bucked you up. She abandoned the teapot, which was cooling down anyway, and went into the sitting-room.

The radio was indulging itself with a jazzy version of an Offenbach waltz.

Then the doorbell rang. Just once, but long and loud.

Stella hesitated, then slowly made her way to the front door. Her legs felt weak. She peered through the spy-hole.

No one. The quadrangle was empty.

Keeping the chain on the door, she opened it. 'Who's there?'

No answer came from the night.

She went back in and turned the radio down so that she could listen. Now it was announcing that the traffic diversion on the Lower Road was over and traffic was flowing freely.

This time Stella did pour out some whisky and had the glass to her lips when the bell rang again. Twice.

She drank her whisky deliberately, ignoring the bell. Then the ringing started again, rhythmically. Long, short, short, long. And again.

Drink in hand, Stella went to the door and peered out through the hole.

Four youths circled her door, mouthing silently at her. She could not make out the words. There were no words, they were just mouthing obscenely.

She backed away from the door, towards the sitting-room. They couldn't get inside. Then she heard the noise of breaking glass behind her.

Her heart was banging in her throat as she turned to meet him. She had guessed he would be there. Coming through the door from the bathroom, in jeans and a dirty sweatshirt, the one with the teeth, the one she had met before, the one she feared.

'You didn't quite shut your bathroom window, lady, so I've come on through it to protect you.'

A smell of smoke and sour sweat had come into the room with him.

'Get out.' She looked at Bob who had risen up from the sofa, growling. 'I'll call the police.' But he was between her and the telephone.

'Shouldn't bother. You asked me in, you left the window open for me.'

'It wasn't open. You broke in.'

He shrugged. 'It's what I say that counts. You know what the police are like? Men, like me. They'll believe me... Did you like my diversionary band outside? They said they'd make a nice show while I came through. So you wouldn't hear me. I wanted to surprise you.'

He'd done that all right. Stella rallied her forces. 'Well, you've done that, now get out.'

'Of course, I could ask them in, and then you'd have all of us. Or all of us could have you.'

Stella tried to reach for the telephone, but he got a grip on her arm. 'But I don't want to spoil it for myself.' He put one arm round her waist, holding her tightly. A knife appeared in his right hand.

In spite of herself, she gave a small scream. She threw her drink in his face, he swore at her and knocked the glass from her hand.

Bob leapt forward, growling and snapping. Toothface kicked at him hard, and Bob yelped and retreated with blood coming from his jaws. Then Toothface turned his attention to Stella, pulling at her jeans, tearing the thin silk pants underneath with the one hand while holding the knife to her throat.

'Unzip me.'

Stella did nothing.

'You're a cow, lady, I thought that the first time I saw you and I thought: I know what I'd like to do to that cow.' He pressed the knife against her face, just above the mouth. 'Unzip me. I like it that way.'

Slowly, Stella did as he asked.

'Now, baby, now.'

I'm an actress, Stella thought, Act, for your life. Virtue didn't really seem to matter so much, getting stabbed did.

'I'm not frightened of you,' she managed to say. 'I'm theatre, remember. I've seen better things than your rather pink and puffy member.' He hit her hard in the face. 'Pig.' She managed to get contempt in her voice. Come on, Egypt, she commanded herself, Royal Egypt, forward Lady Macbeth, up Clytemnestra.

All the same, she did not seem able to resist what appeared to be happening to her. She seemed to be being pressed against the table, she could smell sweat. What's going to happen, she asked herself, am I going to enjoy this bloody process?

The radio was still playing and even at that moment she found herself able to take in the announcer's voice saying that the siege in Elder Street was over with no casualties. Fred Kinver had surrendered.

Toothface had said nothing, she had already summed him up as someone who would not be able to have an orgasm and talk at the same time, but the obtrusive teeth were cutting into her lips.

Summoning up all the suppleness and muscular strength that long years of theatre exercises had given her, she arched her back, got her face a few crucial inches away, then leant forward and bit his nose.

He screamed. Suddenly the knife was on the floor. She kicked it away, and bit him again.

They were on the floor, rolling against each other. He was grabbing at her, forcing her legs apart. She hit his face and started to shout for help.

Bob, suddenly brave again, leapt upon them, barking wildly. There was blood over both of them.

Whether it was coming from Bob, him or her did not seem clear.

A puzzling smell of smoke and burning was coming in from outside.

I'm not going to get out of this, Stella thought. All the same, she managed to edge her hand nearer to the knife.

JOHN COFFIN heard the news about the fire at St Luke's over the radio of a patrol car as he stood in the precinct of the police station congratulating Inspector Lee on the successful ending of the Kinver siege. Both the Kinvers had been admitted to hospital for observation.

'A fire reported at St Luke's Mansions, old St Luke's Street. A break-in suspected. Car and fire brigade on the way.'

As Coffin was driven there himself, they were passed by a car full of young men going the other way and leaning out of the car and shouting.

When he got to St Luke's, the fire in the quadrangle was already under control.

'A window is broken at the back,' reported the man from the patrol car.

'That's Stella Pinero's place,' said someone else. Lily's party members were crowding round.

'I rang the bell. No answer, sir,' said the patrol man. 'Shall I break the door down?'

Coffin hesitated only for a moment. 'I have the key,' he said.

He put the key in the lock, the chain was on, and, full of fear, he and the constable shouldered the door to break a way through.

As he did so Stella staggered out towards him and he put his arms round her. 'I don't think I've killed that chap, but I might have done. Thank God it's all over.'

He looked around him at the blood and confusion. Not quite, he thought. This might be, but there is still the murder of Anna Mary Kinver.

# SEVENTEEN

*Thursday, June 29, in daylight. Then on into July*

DURING THE NIGHT, the streets of Leathergate and Spinnergate were cleared of the wreckage of the night before and then they were washed. A faint odour of disinfectant hung over some streets where the trouble had been greatest and messiest. The paving stones on the floor of the quadrangle in St Luke's Mansions were blackened by the fire, but the architect and his builder, who had viewed it, said they could easily be replaced. There was just a small stained area by Stella's front door, as if someone had deliberately marked it, that might be difficult to remove and which thus would remain there as a permanent memorial to her experience.

Coffin had taken Stella to his own flat after a police surgeon had examined her, and there she had spent the night.

In the morning, accompanied by Bob, who was minus several teeth, he took her some breakfast in bed. Leaning against the pillows, she looked tired and a little battered but cheerful.

'I believe I am going to have a black eye.' She drank some coffee. 'But why me?'

'You stand out, Stella. And you were there, that's why.' Also, you can be aggressive, but this was not the time to say so.

'He didn't really do anything, you know. I defy any man to achieve maximum penetration with a dog on his back chewing his ear.'

'Especially when he is getting his nose bitten as well . . . You didn't damage the lout, by the way, the knife wound you gave him was a scratch. Most of the blood came from his nose and from Bob. We'll get his DNA profile, though, it might come in useful.'

'What about . . .' Then she stopped. A question had to be asked but she was frightened.

'No, he was not HIV positive,' said Coffin quickly.

'Thank goodness.'

'I should have told you that at once.'

'It ought to have been funny,' said Stella, 'but by God, it wasn't.'

'I should think not.' He still felt both sick and furious at what had happened to Stella. His Stella.

'Nor enjoyable.'

Coffin gave her a surprised look. 'Did you think it would be?'

Very carefully, Stella put down her cup and took his hand. 'No, silly talk. Thanks for everything.'

'I've sheltered you from a lot of police life, Stella. But it's a rough, cruel world out there and you can get trampled on.'

'I am saying thank you.'

'And I heard. There's a lot of things we've got to talk about, but the Zeman affair is over, cleared up. Nastily but effectively. No more Paper Man. I'll tell you all about it later. But meanwhile there's someone I've got to see.'

DR FELICITY ZEMAN was alone in the house in Feather Street. She was surrounded by flowers, brought in and

arranged by her friends in Feather Street, Phil Darbyshire and Mary Anneck leading the band. She need
not cook a meal for weeks, her freezer had been filled.
Or she could come to them? Felicity was to say. She
had not been one of them, but now she was welcome
to join the sisterhood, they would be glad. A little
overwhelmed by such friendliness, Felicity was happy
to be alone. Some griefs need silence and solitude, she
thought, and I hope they never have to know it.

Nevertheless, she welcomed John Coffin. With
some humour, she said: 'Would you like some coffee? Or blackberry cordial? Or damson gin? I can also
offer you shortbread, banana cake, and gingerbread.'

He refused all these. 'Just had breakfast. A bit late
this morning.'

'You had quite a night from what I hear.'

He smiled. 'You could say so. But I thought you'd
be glad to see me, and I needed to talk to you. You
know how things stand?'

She nodded. 'Inspector Young and Superintendent
Lane came in person to see me earlier this morning.
Jim's in custody, I believe?' Coffin nodded. 'It's a
shock to know he hated us so much.'

In Jim Marsh's bedroom the police had discovered
videos called *Brain Warrior* and *The Double Man*, so
they knew where he had got some of his ideas.

'A psychopath, I'm afraid, with a lot of hate inside
him.' Coffin shook his head. 'Very cold and manipu-
lative. And of course, he blamed his father for his
mother's death.'

'It's ironic that it was his own father who probably
saved my husband's life.'

'I think Jim hates him for that.'

Felicity said, 'I think he did love Anna Mary Kinver in his way. And he did find her body, one has to remember that. It must have been a terrible shock when it was the girl he admired and loved.'

'Yes, and thought Fred Kinver ill-treated her, which he may have done. A lot of darkness there, I'm afraid. But it is about her death I want to talk. I think you've got something to tell me.'

He waited. Then prompted her: 'Tim did have some guilt to bear, didn't he?'

'How did you know?'

'I guessed. Picked it up. Policemen get the trick. I think Val Humberstone knew a bit and you know all there was to know. He must have told someone, and it had to be you.'

Felicity said: 'Not all, I don't know all. I can't tell you what Tim would have said. I can only tell you how he told it to me.' She got up, hugging Arthur to her. 'I think we will have some coffee.'

'Jim Marsh accused Tim of the murder.'

Felicity took a deep breath. 'I think I can guess that Tim would have accepted that responsibility. Although not of the actual killing.' She put some coffee on the stove to heat. 'Parents and children . . . it's difficult?' She made it a query.

'I know,' said Coffin, thinking of his own wandering mother whose diary was presently giving him such a problem. To publish, as Letty wanted, or not?'

'Perhaps if Timmy had got on better with his father. Or I had been a better mother . . . One blames oneself, but it might be genetic. Or should one just accept that people, even one's own children, have a right to be what they want?'

'I think that's the best solution,' said Coffin gravely. His parent had just dumped him and left. That was voting with your feet, if you liked.

'Anyway, after experimenting a bit, Tim decided where his sexual tastes lay. He talked to Anna Mary, she helped him there. Probably physically, but I'm not sure about that. I hardly knew her, but I think she must have been a sensitive and loving girl. She understood, although I believe she loved Tim. That's sad, isn't it?' Coffin nodded to her. 'Of course, she wasn't without experience.'

Coffin waited for Felicity to continue her story.

'He told me all this afterwards, you understand? I said he must talk to you or someone like you, but he was so frightened. He'd had a bad time with your Inspector and there was a lot of hostility towards him on all sides. Well, you know that yourself... I think he would have told you in the end.'

'What would he have told me? I have a few ideas myself.'

'A day or so before what happened in Rope Alley, he met a boy. About his own age, seventeen or eighteen, maybe older, and he was violently attracted. Fell in love, I suppose I'd have to say. It was the first time it had happened to him in such a strong, physical way... He didn't know how to handle it.'

'Difficult at any time,' said Coffin with sympathy. It could strike anyone, that particular virus, and was always painful.

'He thought the boy liked him back. First approaches seemed welcome. But they had a sort of quarrel. Tim went off that day to visit friends, to think things over, he said... As you know, he came back.'

'And he didn't spend all the time that evening he said he did sitting in a park?'

'No. He went to the disco where he knew the lad would be. I think by that time they had both had something to drink. Drugs too, possibly, although Timmy swore this was not so in his case... This time he was bold enough to make a direct approach to the boy.'

'So?'

'The boy, young man really, was savage. Taunted Tim, screamed at him. According to Tim, it was more than just anger. Frenzy. And then he yelled at Tim that he was going out to get a girl. "I'm going out to get a girl," those were his words.' She covered her eyes for a moment. 'And he did. He got Anna Mary Kinver.'

There was a moment's silence.

She looked up. 'I suppose you'll never get him now?'

'Oh, I believe we might,' said Coffin. 'You see, Anna Mary named him.'

Felicity looked up in surprise. 'Oh, but...' she started to say.

'No, not Zeman, but seaman. He was a seaman, and I think Sir Harry got his photograph.' And a man called Solomon Wild, now undergoing treatment for a mental illness, might have been a witness to the quarrel and then the murder. Coffin had him down for questioning. 'I think her killer was off one of the ships on the river that day. A few small vessels still come up-river, but not many, which makes our task easier. I believe we will get him.'

SOME WEEKS LATER, after much patient work, police in the port of Rotterdam boarded the small vessel, SS

*Don Romolo*, flying under a flag of convenience. Inspector Archie Young was among them with the correct papers to detain and arrest his suspect.

They went to the cabin of one of the young seamen, a Dutch boy called Vannie. He was sitting on his bunk, reading a comic. He looked surprised to see the police and frightened.

He was taken away for questioning. Inspector Archie Young asked for certain specimens of body fluid to be taken. He knew he had got his killer.

Because before they had left his cabin, it had been searched. When a locker on the wall was opened, out fell half a dozen women's shoes.

One was small and silvery, one of the pair that Anna Mary Kinver had bought the night of her death.

Vannie looked at it and started to mumble. 'I must have one shoe,' he said. 'Always I have to get a shoe. Always.'

Tears stared to pour down his face. 'Always before she let me have a shoe when we made love, but that night no. No, to everything, because of the silver shoes.'

Poor Anna Mary, poor little Cinderella, killed for a silver shoe.

THUS THE CASE started with the code word GRIM had at last wound to its conclusion.